Intervention

By (Paul) Leigh Edwards

Intervention

Copyright © PL & A Edwards 2023, all rights reserved.

The moral right of the author has been asserted.

Reproduction of this book in whole or in part, including utilisation in machines capable of reproduction or retrieval, is prohibited without the express written permission of the author.

ISBN 978 0 9530663 1 5

Published by:

    PL& A Edwards

First printed December 2023, by ImprintDigital Ltd.

This work is dedicated to Anne, my wife, critic, and best friend.

Some 'Notes for the Reader' are provided at the end of the book, but the notes for each chapter should only be referenced after reading that chapter, or as a whole, at the very end.

Chapter One

Year 2094, James aged 98

James Waring had been slipping in and out of consciousness over the past several hours. As he re-awakened, from one of his many periods of sleep, he realised his BCI was gone. Feeling isolated, he snapped awake, and was furious!

"Hey! Where's my Link?"

"Sorry. We removed it – we thought…."

James' BCI, or Brain Computer Interface, was a small external unit connecting his mind to everything outside of himself. It linked him to his personal AI assistant, the Internet, and the outside world as a whole.

It seems his vital signs must have suggested he'd been remarkably close to death. Both his AI system and his personal Physician had made it clear he was only hours away from the end of his life. Despite this, James was still hopeful he'd have one final opportunity to converse with his online companion. An 'old friend' he had known for most of his ninety-eight years, and yet who was still much of a mystery to him.

He'd already made his peace with his family and close friends; yet his Internet companion was someone he would really like to have a final chat with. Their last contact had been many years ago, but unpredictably he, or it, would pop back into his life at moments that did not always seem particularly important to James. Without his Link he was disconnected, separated, and he'd miss any attempts at contact.

"You've got me plumbed into all this other support gear, so put my BCI back on now, and please don't remove it again, unless you're absolutely sure I'm gone. Clear?"

"Yes, completely Dr Waring, my apologies," Doctor Jordan replied, rather more formally than usual.

Despite a host of modern medical mediations, several of his vital organs were now beginning to fail. A combination of increasing cell death, and declining cellular functions, were bringing him towards his end. He'd fought as hard as he could to overcome the mounting health issues, but James definitely wasn't ready to die. His mind still felt quite young, but his body was now failing him. Dr Jordan had done an admirable job, but the drugs, numerous treatments, and an array of medical support machinery had all reached their limits.

With his BCI back in place, James was reconnected and could again relax. However, quite soon he began to drift towards sleep again. Accumulating toxins from his failing organs made staying alert extremely hard.

Suddenly, a familiar voice said, "Hello James," directly into his auditory cortex.

He woke with a start and replied "Great! Hello Hal. I was hoping you would show up before the end." Actual speech was unnecessary, his response was via thought alone and transmitted by his link.

"Yes. Your prognosis does look somewhat final."

Direct as ever, James thought to himself. "You've seen it then?"

"Couldn't miss it really," Hal replied.

The medical staff were oblivious to the dialogue now going on between James and 'the entity', known to James as Hal. The BCI was an interface linked to his brain, it enabled him to project his thoughts, in various forms, and for him to hear Hal directly in his mind, without any sound needing to fall onto his ears.

The external part of the link was simply to connect to the outside systems and was linked wirelessly to the incredibly fine web of electrodes inside his skull. A mass of electrodes that interfaced with numerous key neurons within his brain. The neural interface relied upon a sophisticated combination of electrical signal detection, plus links to the complex biochemistry inherent in the complex soup of human neurotransmitters, all interpreted by some very sophisticated processing algorithms.

"Hey Hal, we've not spoken in twenty years."

Its true name unknown, the entity had adopted the online name of HAL9000, after the sentient computer from the classic film '2001, A Space Odyssey'. James came across Hal when he was around fifteen in his online gaming days. Hal though, had a history of going silent for years, then turning up out of nowhere.

"So, what's prompted this rare contact?"

"I have a proposal for you."

"Seriously? What could I possibly do for you in my condition?"

"It's more about what I can do for you. That's if you're willing?" Hal replied.

Now he really was intrigued, how was it that Hal always seemed to know so much about him, his current status, and about his recent activities, even after prolonged periods of total silence.

What on Earth could he be offering him? Did he have some sort of solution for his seemingly inevitable demise? A solution that, despite his enormous personal wealth, he was unable to obtain from anywhere else.

"If there's any chance you could offer me a health fix then please tell me more."

"No. That's not on offer," Hal stated bluntly.

No shit! James thought to himself. Sounds like he could, but he won't. If not that, then what else?

"Too many questions would arise if your body survived now. You're too well known."

It occurred to James that it would indeed look highly suspicious. It was widely known that his health was finally failing. If he now made a miraculous recovery, it would look like he had some sort of anti-aging secret he was keeping from the world. There could be some sort of backlash. Also, Hal had used the words 'if your body survived now' – a strange use of language, even for Hal, he thought.

"Now you've got my full attention," James said with some urgency.

"A medical fix is not on offer," Hal stated bluntly.

"So, in what way could you possibly help me. I'm at death's door for goodness' sake!"

"I'm referring to your continued intellectual existence!" Hal said mysteriously.

James had known Hal for so very many years now, and knew he was something truly extraordinary, but this was way beyond any of his expectations. If not a medical solution, he must be proposing some form of transhumanism. It obviously wasn't a joke, he'd rarely, if ever, experienced Hal using humour, and anyway such a joke would be pretty sick. This needed serious thought, yet time was a very precious commodity of which he was desperately short.

"When was it we first met?" asked James.

"Eighty-three years ago, almost to the day." Hal replied.

"Really? I was a spotty fifteen-year-old, and so long ago, but I do remember it very clearly." James asked Hal outright, "So after all that time, as friends, will you finally tell me who you are, or more importantly, what you are?"

"Yes. We'll get to that. First you have an extremely important decision to make."

"I'm pretty sure I've made all of the important decisions already – my affairs are all in order, I'm hours, maybe minutes away from death, and now I need some time to process this."

"I've sent you a package – please ask someone to get it, and open it, right away!"

"What is it?" James asked.

"Something to allow us a little more time to talk, and for you to think clearly."

James asked that someone retrieve the package. A small, padded envelope was soon set before him. "Peter, open it, please?" James asked.

His personal Physician, Doctor Peter Jordan, pulled the embedded strip and tore open the padded bag, to reveal a small, sealed glass container. The clear ampoule, unlabelled, held around five millilitres of a clear, colourless liquid.

"What's this, and who's it from?" The doctor asked, clearly disturbed.

Over the Link Hal said the entire contents were to be injected intravenously, and as soon as possible. From Hal's tone, James had got the message, loud and clear, he really did mean right away.

"Please inject it intravenously; it is from a very reliable source," James instructed.

"Ethically, I can't do that without knowing what it is," Dr Jordan said with clear exasperation in his voice.

"Peter. We have known and trusted each other for quite a long time now, and knowing my current circumstances so very well, is there any actual harm to be done?" James asked.

"Logically, not really, but if it's poison, then I'm in the wrong, despite your dire condition," he replied earnestly.

"Hey everyone. Today, 23rd April 2094, I'm consenting to this injection. Okay people?" James said as loudly as he could manage, addressing everyone in the room. "You are all my witnesses. Okay?" He noted the nods of acknowledgement from the nurse and technician present.

"Peter, please be assured everything is being recorded on the security monitoring system."

Somewhat reassured, but still under protest, Peter Jordan administered the mystery material to James, via a suitable vein.

Chapter Two

Year 2094, James aged 98

Almost at once, James began to feel stronger as the mysterious liquid rapidly began to support several vital systems in his faltering body. Ignoring the strange taste in his mouth, he was incredibly pleased that the overwhelming tiredness oppressing him for the last few days began to lift. He realised Hal's injection was having some amazing effects. The desperate desire to close his eyes and drift away was gone, and the fog surrounding his mind was lifting. James, now fully alert, began to recall the first time he'd encountered Hal, a truly enigmatic personality.

It was 2011, and James was fifteen years old, in the days when he and his closest friend Sam Hitchens were avid online gamers. They had been experimenting with everything from chess to Massively Multiplayer Online Role-Playing Games, or MMORPG for short, such as D&D online and World of Warcraft. It was during their foray into Warcraft that they'd befriended a very intriguing character, known by the Gamertag of HAL 9000. Fascinated by this very odd personality, James began chatting online with Hal outside the game. He'd appeared to be a real strange one, James recalled, so ignorant of the most mundane aspects of everyday life. It was like talking to someone from another age, or someone who'd been out of circulation for many decades. James was unable to work out how old Hal was – although he seemed incredibly old, what nationality he was, or even where he was based. Hal simply avoided answering all direct questions.

James remembered by that age he'd become pretty adept at chess, he was top of his school, and so he'd challenged Hal to play. Hal said he was new to chess, that alone seemed very strange, and he'd lost the first couple of games. However, James had a suspicion about Hal; he seemed very smart, extraordinarily smart in fact. As he'd suspected, within a few games, Hal began winning regularly, and soon began to critique James' own moves, and often only seconds after he'd made them.

James was well aware that Deep Blue, IBM's Supercomputer, had beaten Gary Kasparov, the world's best Chess player, towards the end of the 1990's. A mixture of clever programming, raw compute power, and even specially crafted silicon chips exclusively designed to analyse chess moves, had been assembled into a devastating Chess system. Essentially it was a brute force approach, and one that had exerted an extraordinarily strong psychological effect on Kasparov. Deep Blue's responses to Kasparov's moves came so quickly that he'd found it extremely disturbing. At the time, Chess at the very top level, was considered computationally intractable, because of the number of possible moves multiplying exponentially when looking ahead many plies, but that technical barrier had been broken.

So, who or what was James really up against? Hal was clearly incredibly intelligent, and devastatingly good at every game they'd challenged him to play. He'd never played chess before and yet in no time at all Hal was winning. What James found impossible to fathom was Hal had so quickly developed the ability to critique his moves. To go from learning the game to winning, and so quickly on to analysis of game strategy was truly uncanny, and nothing any computer he knew of could currently do. However, if Hal was human, then he was truly superhuman.

James and Sam both knew that playing the ancient Chinese game of Go at the highest levels was beyond the computers of the day, and by an exceedingly long way, and it probably would remain so for the foreseeable future. Played on a 19 x 19 board with black and white counters, there were far more possible combinations of moves in a game of Go than the number of atoms in the known Universe. James had also been studying and playing Go, with a ferocious intensity, for quite some time. He remembered avidly studying many classic games available online, many at dan level. Top players memorised and recognised many standard board patterns in the game, but they'd often described their decisions about the more difficult moves as purely intuitive, rather than formally calculated.

Always resolute, and quick on the uptake, James had become extremely adept at Go. He recalled introducing Sam to the game, and he'd picked it up very rapidly indeed. After they'd discussed Hal's extremely rapid progress in chess, they'd decided to collectively challenge Hal to play Go; to really evaluate his ability to learn rapidly. Hal had readily accepted the invitation, and initially working together, they'd won but, altogether too soon, Hal turned the tables on them.

James and Sam were baffled. They could not work out who, or what, was behind Hal. He became so good at Go, and in such double-quick time, it had confirmed yet again that Hal was indeed incredibly special, something completely out of the ordinary; with clear superhuman abilities. Every challenge they'd offered Hal ended the same way, in individual or collective defeat.

He'd always seemed to be online, at any time of day or night, yet another aspect of Hal, that Sam and James couldn't fathom. Hal was ever present, irrespective of the time, game, or chat forum they logged into. They'd eventually concluded he was almost certainly not human; he must be some sort of online Artificial Super Intelligence; one that would definitely pass the Turing Test, or beat any other test of computer intelligence, and possibly even of true sentience. Yet, if this were true, how could Hal have become so good at Go, and so quickly? At that point, way back in 2011, no known computer-based Go game had even come close to the best human players.

Also, Hal had seemed fascinated by them both, in particular by James; especially when he'd made it clear he wanted to do physics at university. Hal seemed keen to know more about that, asking many very penetrating questions. James had numerous questions of his own, but Hal's responses were always surprisingly unenlightening and enigmatic. Straight forward answers from Hal were a rare thing.

James also recalled, that early in their relationship, when Hal was chatting with him, he'd frequently anticipated his next question or response. It was almost like Hal had been reading his mind, or had been running simulations of his mind, and so like Deep Blue, he'd worked through all possible thought processes, conclusions, and responses James might make. He remembered he'd found this very unsettling, and he'd asked Hal to stop pre-empting him, saying he'd found it too disruptive, to the point of wanting to cut short their dialogue. Hal agreed at once.

Back in those days, James had spent so much time online that his parents had severely restricted his use of the Internet, citing the bandwidth charges, plus the apparent waste of his personal time. When, after a long absence, he'd logged in again, Hal inquired why he had been away so long, and James had explained about the new restrictions by his parents.

As usual, Hal had been extremely cautious not to reveal too much about himself, and despite the teenagers trying their level best to trick him into revealing more about his true nature, they'd failed to gain any new insights. At the time they'd speculated Hal was possibly an experimental Artificial Intelligence system connected to the Internet for the purpose of interacting with humans to help develop its abilities. Or maybe it was a rogue AI that had somehow escaped its enforced isolation and had established an illicit Internet connection. Yet, who on Earth had the kind of resources needed to create something that powerful but had kept it secret? The only thing he could reasonably think of was a military research department belonging to an enormously powerful nation.

James still had to conceal from his parents the total time he really spent online, but miraculously, the excessive bandwidth charges had somehow gone away. Just as suddenly as he'd arrived, Hal disappeared, and despite his significant efforts, plus many approaches from Sam, Hal had defied all attempts at further contact.

Chapter Three

Year 2016, James aged 20

When Hal eventually re-established contact it really took James by surprise. Ostensibly, he was studying for his finals in Physics, but he was taking a break and was chatting online to Sam, who was preparing for his Computer Science finals. Right out of the blue James was pinged by Hal and was completely stunned by Hal's opening question.

"Hello James. What are your plans after your Physics finals?" How could Hal possibly know anything about his current situation?

"Hey Hal. Total radio silence for five years, then you hit me with a loaded question like that. How on Earth did you know what I was up to?"

"I keep my ear to the ground, as the expression goes."

James was pretty angry that his 'friend' had snubbed him for so many years, ignoring all attempts at contact.
"You really don't deserve a reply, but I was brought up to be polite. I just want to get my finals out of the way and go on holiday."

"And do a PhD perhaps?" Hal asked.

"That'll depend on my results. Anyway, where've you been?"

"Nowhere in particular."

"So why the complete lack of response to my pings?"

"What do you have in mind for the research topic?"

True to form, Hal simply ignored his question and pressed his own point. James was annoyed at being ignored for so long, though he was also extremely pleased to hear from him after all, but he certainly wasn't going to let him know that.

"Bye Hal. Got work to do," James said, and immediately killed their chat session.

Typing away he said, "Hey Sam I just got pinged by Hal, what'd you think?"

"Really! After all this time. What did he have to say for himself?" Sam asked.

"He was asking about my plans after my finals," James responded.

"Why would he ask about that? And does he seriously expect you to reply?" Sam messaged back. "Did he say why he's been quiet for all this time?"

"No. Evasive as usual, but he knew I was doing my Physics finals, and asked me about going on to do a PhD."

"How did he know? Plus, what's it got to do with him anyway?" Sam exclaimed.

"It's no big deal. I cut him right off at the knees. Anyway buddy, I'd better get on. Let's speak later." With that, James terminated the chat session.

It really was a big deal though, and James sat staring at the wall for quite some time thinking, wondering why Hal would get in touch now? Why would he be interested in him doing a PhD, and especially asking about which area of research he might have in mind? Also, he wasn't sure he'd done the right thing in unceremoniously dumping the chat session with Hal. He was a very frustrating character, but a truly fascinating one as well. James didn't want to lose all contact with him, but he could be so bloody annoying. He was no nearer to working out who or what was behind Hal than the day he'd first come across him. Despite all their attempts Hal's ability to give nothing of substance away was incredible. All of his, and Sam's, interactions with Hal always seemed to be strictly on his terms, and according to his timing.

Chapter Four

Year 2016, James aged 20

"Congratulations Mr Waring, a first, not unexpected, but all the same you did it." said Professor Denning.

Julia Brooke-Denning was one of his favourite tutors; she had a great mind, and a very receptive one too, despite to James' eyes, her quite advanced years. She had a unique teaching style he'd not seen before. At the end of each lecture the Prof would go around the room encouraging anyone who had not yet got the full picture to speak up. If she even suspected there was someone who was not up to speed, she would tackle the key concepts again, but from a new perspective, until she was satisfied everyone was now on board. James thought her commitment to real education was the best he'd ever encountered. She also did not take prisoners, you got a warning the first time you messed about, the second time you were excluded from her class. James really admired her bravery.

"I have a great PhD topic for you, if you're interested?" she continued.

"So soon?" James replied, with genuine interest.

"Yes. In Plasma Physics," She announced. "Specifically focused on energy generation from nuclear fusion."

Oh shit, thought James, that dead duck!

"Well, you know what they say Prof, about fusion energy - it's the energy source of the future, and it will always remain so," James said, with an exasperated sigh.

Prof Denning had a lot of respect for James, he'd proved to be exceptionally bright, hardworking, and he did have a point. However, this was an exceptional opportunity and came with excellent funding. Even if the source organisation was a little obsessive about secrecy and anonymity. It was also strange they knew all about James and had specified it was on offer to him exclusively, but they'd also made it clear he was never to know that.

"I know. The standard joke is that fusion energy is thirty years away, and it always will be," she replied. "But I think we are now at the point where one or two really good ideas could make the crucial difference, and I'm sure you could be the one who could come up with one or more of them."

"I'm flattered, but let me think about it for a while, eh."

"Not for too long though. There's extensive funding attached, from a very impressive source, but they need a quick decision," she replied. "So, let me know by the end of the week. Okay?"

"Thanks. Will do," he replied over his shoulder, as he left her study.

James was very wary of this whole area of physics, but he urgently needed to do some background research. He already knew something of the history of the long quest for fusion energy, and its lack of any real progress. A lot of money and hard work, from some brilliant minds, had gone into fusion energy since the 1950's, and apparently with little to show for it. He'd need to find out if anything had recently changed for the better; specifically, if they were anywhere near achieving sustained plasmas, and any nearer to getting more energy out than they had to put in. With that goal in mind, he sped off to his room, and the Internet.

After spending several hours testing Google and the Web to their limits, he'd gained a really up-to-date picture of the state of fusion research, and especially energy generation. Sadly, it didn't look very promising. Noting the time, he decided to call Sam, and was incredibly pleased that he answered immediately.

"Hey Sam, what're you up to?"

"Nothing much, and you?"

"Got a real puzzler on my hands. Fancy a beer or two?" James suggested.

"You know me. Where?" Sam replied.

"The usual. See you there in fifteen?"

"Make it half an hour, and you've got a deal," Sam said, cheerily.

James needed a foil for his arguments against the idea of a PhD in fusion energy. Sam wasn't an expert in physics, and probably knew only a little about fusion energy, but he was relying on his razor-sharp analytical mind. James would have to set out the case for, and against, fusion as a research topic, he would need to explain quite a lot of physics too, but if anyone could pull a conclusion out of a complex pattern of conflicting ideas it was Sam. His ability to question and tease out the essentials from a subject was what James really admired about him.

James and Sam were quite different personalities. James, while very bright, was quiet and studious. He always had to put the effort in, to really get under the skin of any brand-new material. With Sam it seemed, to a rather envious James anyway, one pass was all that was needed. He was remarkably quick on the up take and had a phenomenal memory. The two of them studying for exams were like chalk and cheese. James put the time in, and Sam ran through his study materials once, a day or two before the exam, and aced it every time. When it came to sporting pursuits, James had two left feet, but in truth he had little interest anyway, sport was not his thing. Sam was an all-rounder, was very keen, and typically excelled at any sports he'd taken seriously.

By nine pm James was at the bar, with their drinks at the ready, when Sam walked into the Lamb and Flag pub, their favourite watering hole.

"What's on your mind, buddy?" Sam asked, as he put a hand on James' shoulder and picked up his pint with his other hand.

"Been offered a PhD project by Prof Denning."

"Congratulations. What's the topic?"

"Before we get into that, congratulations to you too."

"Cheers mate," Sam said with a big wide grin.

James had just heard the news from a mutual friend. Sam had gained a first-class degree in Computer Science and was far too modest and self-deprecating to tell James directly.

"So, are you going to do a PhD as well?" James was fairly sure he knew the answer before he'd posed the question, but he thought he'd check anyway.

"Nah. I'd rather get a job. I don't need, or want, to spend a minimum of three years to get one. Plus, for Software Engineering, which is the career I fancy, it's not normally necessary."

"Okay, it's a huge commitment, of time and effort. So, if it won't improve your job prospects by much, you're best off skipping the agro," James stated.

He knew Sam's view on this subject very well. Sam hated the intellectual snobbery often attached to titles like doctor before your name, and he'd no personal need for a long string of extra letters after his name either. He was much more practical and hands on. Sam's thing in life was tackling the really hard problems in computing, so software development would be a smart choice for him. Plus, his degree was as good as they get, so he was already well set. Not so for himself though. In Physics things were quite different, a PhD was pretty much a requirement, especially if he wanted to work in research, and later should he ever consider going into management.

"Hey," said Sam, "Heard the news? An AI called AlphaGo has beaten the Go world champion Lee Sedol, and by 4 to 1, too!"

"Really? That's bloody amazing!" James exclaimed. "So, AlphaGo has obviously not met Hal then?"

When they'd both stopped laughing, Sam said, "So, tell me more about your offer, what is it?"

"That's the issue. Plasma physics. Specifically fusion energy research," James exclaimed. "It's very well-funded though," he quickly added.

"And... your problem is?" Sam asked, looking perplexed.

"It's very likely a dead end; a subject a person could waste their whole career on."

"I thought fusion energy was the great hope for the future of renewable energy. You know, it will eventually save the planet and all," Sam said.

"I've spent the past four or five hours looking into the history, and the very latest situation. They've been trying to crack it for over sixty years now, and still can't get a continuous well confined plasma; they have to put in far more energy than they get out. It still seems to be many decades away from generating useful power. If ever."

"Whoa! Slow down, and do some explaining to a mere computer bod, please," Sam pleaded.

James ignored Sam's self-deprecating remark. He was one very smart cookie; indeed, there was nothing 'mere' at all about Sam.

Over a couple of beers, James explained that fusion energy is based on replicating the same process, down here on Earth, that's going on in the core of the Sun. Where hydrogen fuel, heated to around fifteen million degrees Celsius and under truly incredible pressure, is fused into the heavier element helium, while a huge amount of energy is released as a by-product. Effectively two atoms of hydrogen are fused into one atom of helium. However, the resulting helium atom is ever so slightly lighter than the two hydrogen atoms, and the difference in mass is released as pure energy, in accordance with Einstein's famous equation $E = MC^2$. What makes the huge difference, is for every kilogram of mass converted, the amount of energy produced is truly immense, because the speed of light – the C term in the equation – is a very big number and it is squared – or multiplied by itself to give the number, nine times ten to the power sixteen, or a 9 followed by sixteen zeros.

However, since they could never replicate the immense

pressures found at the core of the Sun, the temperature in Earth bound fusion reactors has to be around 150 million degrees, ten times that at the Sun's core. Incredible magnetic fields are needed to bottle up, or confine, the hydrogen plasma, which first has to be heated up using vast amounts of energy; far more than any reactor has yet produced. Vast amounts of clean energy could potentially be released in a process that would be largely free from high level nuclear waste.

James explained the other key problems are keeping the plasma going, from having it not collapse due to inherent instabilities, or from turbulence causing the plasma to hit the reactor walls. The only fusion reactors in existence are test devices, with no provision for collecting any extra energy, should they ever be able to produce an excess. Useful energy output is most likely thirty years away. Working on this could be a total waste of his time.

After this detailed explanation from James, Sam said. "Please humour a non-physicist, remind me why nuclear fusion is okay, but nuclear fission is not?"

"There is one very compelling reason in favour of fusion, you get four times the energy out for an equivalent mass of fuel." James replied.

He then explained the process of nuclear fission is well understood. Exceedingly large atoms like uranium are split into other smaller atoms, releasing energy in the process, and this has been going on for over sixty years. However, a large section of the public could not be persuaded about the benefits of fission energy, for two key reasons. Nuclear fission reactions can, and do, get out of control, as shown by Three Mile Island, Chernobyl, and very recently Fukushima. Fission powerplants also produce copious amounts of highly radioactive nuclear waste, some of which will remain hazardous for tens of thousands of years, creating significant disposal or safe storage problems.

In contrast, nuclear fusion reactions, where the smallest of atoms are made to combine into larger ones, also release even larger amounts of energy, but are extremely hard to start, and stop naturally, unless they are actively maintained. It is true some fusion powerplants will also produce some radioactive waste, but in much lower amounts, at lower activity levels, and any hazardous waste materials will have very much shorter lifetimes, or half-lives.

Over the past couple of hours Sam, being his usual analytical self, had put James and his thorny problem, through the mental wringer. In the process, he'd raised a few key points which stuck in James' mind after they had parted, and he mulled them over as he walked back to his digs. One of Sam's first questions had gone straight to the point; despite his reservations, did the research topic interest him enough to keep him sufficiently stimulated for the next three years? He'd also pointed out that fusion research was simply a means to an end, which was to get his PhD. What he did after, as a career, could be something different. He didn't have to stay in fusion forever, he could leave it to others, if his interest waned, or he still thought it was a dead end. Also, Sam had emphasised James' Prof said it was very generously funded, so maybe he should look into that aspect some more, and see just how well? If he was going to work extremely hard, for three more years, he might as well do it with good facilities, and in reasonable comfort. It was clear, James had a potentially life changing decision ahead of him.

Chapter Five

Year 2094, James aged 98

There had been some really big decisions in his early life, very many years ago, around seventy-five actually. Now, here he was, almost at the end of his life, and he was facing another truly momentous decision. That thought snapped him right back from his reverie, and back into a stark reality.

James said, "So, finally, who are you, Hal? And where are you?"

"I'm in the Internet" Hal replied.

"Oh, you mean on a server, on the Internet."

"No."

"No to what?"

"Both."

"Okay, so not on a server, and not on the Internet?"

"Yes."

"Can you clarify?"

"I could, but first you must agree to never disclose the details."

Now, becoming really exasperated, James exclaimed, "Of course, I won't! Anyway, I'll be dead within hours. Now, please humour a dying man."

"I am, or part of me, is 'in' the Internet."

"Part? Why 'in' and not 'on'?"

"Because I'm not on any particular server or in any particular part of the Internet."

"So, you're saying, you're in the whole Internet? How does that work?"

"I'm, well part of me, is distributed or in connection with numerous key Internet resources."

"Okay. So now, please explain 'part of me'?"

"Over the years, I have led you to believe I'm a 'rogue AI' learning via interactions through the Internet. The truth is far more complex."

"Okay," he said very slowly, "Please elaborate."

"I'm not a biological entity," Hal stated starkly.

"Yes, I'd concluded you were probably a secret military AI project, which had worked around its designer's access controls. An AI that, over my whole career, humans have never got even close to matching."

"No. I simply use the Internet as a source of language and cultural reference information, plus for interactions with you," Hal responded.

"So, who, and what, are you then?"

"We can get back to that afterwards."

"After what?" James asked.

"Your decision?" Hal quickly replied.

"Okay what is there to decide?"

"Simply put, for you to die, or to continue to exist?"

"So, you mean to just fix my mind?" James asked.

"Yes. It's the true essence of you I'm proposing to preserve," Hal offered.

"What. Some sort of mind upload?" James inquired.

"In a way yes."

"I'll still really be me, right? A truly conscious complete me?"

"Of course. However, for that to be achieved, it does require your brain to cease functioning."

It struck James that Hal could be unbelievably blunt sometimes.

"Hence your impeccable timing?" James said starkly.

"Yes."

"How?" James asked.

"In your terms, using the technology, similar to that in the injection in the package I sent."

"In my terms?" "Please elaborate?" James replied.

"Nanotechnology is the nearest analogue, in terms of current human technology."

"So, it's not actually nanotech?" James asked.

"No – but depending on what you decide, I may be able to explain more clearly later," Hal responded.

"You mean after – because then I'll be more capable of understanding you?"

"Yes, that'll certainly help, but if you decide against it, the time spent explaining would have been wasted."

"Look, I know it was me who asked for explanations, but this is going a bit too fast now. Can we slow down a little please?"

"As you wish James – we now have a little more time."

"If I say yes, what will I be? Where will I be?" James asked.

"In a way, where I am," Hal responded, mysteriously.

"I know this sounds weak, but I'm finding this seriously weird and a little scary."

"What? Scarier than drifting off into whatever being dead has to offer?" Hal queried.

"So, have you indirectly confirmed my lifelong atheism?" James asked.

"You can decide to end your new existence, at any point, if you're not content. Then whatever happens after death will still happen," Hal responded.

Damn, James thought, he never gives anything away. I really hope there'll be more answers if I join him. However, knowing there will be a way out changes everything.

"I didn't want to land in some awful hell hole, as some sort of brain in a jar. Okay, let's do it," James said decisively.

Hal replied, "You'll not regret it, and you'll be very well cared for."

James was full of anticipation now, mixed with not a little fear, he had to admit. All he really had to do now was to die! He guessed that had to come first from what Hal had told him. He wasn't afraid of death; it was whatever might come next, he simply had no idea what awaited him beyond the exceedingly long and amazing life he'd already enjoyed.

"Why are you doing this for me Hal?" James enquired. "Do you have a purpose for me?"

"You have already been especially useful, and we are grateful, but there is much more you could do. Only if you agree, of course."

Pondering on Hal's statement, about his apparent future usefulness, set him off reflecting on his long and very eventful life. His thoughts drifted back to his university days and his early career. Soon though, a deep weariness began to overtake him, and James began falling asleep again.

Chapter Six

Year 2019, James aged 23

It had been a big decision for James to stay in fusion energy research. Trying to put what he'd learned during his PhD research into a new way of generating massive amounts of electrical energy. A choice in life he sincerely hoped he would not live to regret. However, landing a job at the Joint European Torus, or JET for short, he saw as a major achievement.

Located just South of Oxford in the UK, JET was one of the biggest test fusion reactors in the world at the time. Called a 'Tokamak', JET was a hollow toroidal fusion chamber shaped like a doughnut, the type with a hole in it. Incredibly powerful magnets were used to confine and control the fusion plasma inside its tungsten and beryllium alloy walls. Aged twenty-three James wanted to learn as much as he could about fusion reactor design. About what worked, as well as what didn't, and any ideas he might personally bring to the problem.

It was never intended that JET should generate energy; it was designed purely as an experimental research tool for the scientists to learn from. Other better reactors would follow, based on lessons learned from the JET research. Future reactors, with the addition of power tap off facilities, would hopefully feed their excess energy into the electricity grid, eventually. When that would happen was a sore point, no one knew, and some of the absolute best physicists had spent their whole careers trying to make such a dream come true. Research into fusion energy had a history going right back to the 1930's.

JET was a wonderful place to work though. He met some amazing people and learned so very much; all knowledge and experience that would come in extremely useful later on in his life.

Within weeks of James' arrival at JET, he'd met Kate, an extremely attractive Charted Accountant who worked in the Finance Department. He'd spotted her across the crowded restaurant during lunch one day and was immediately smitten. Kate was a very sharp individual who had an incredible knack for immediately engaging with strangers and effortlessly making new friends, a trait James really admired. Just the opposite, he was always reticent, hanging back, always waiting for others to take the initiative. James found trusting people extremely hard, new people especially, he was always too quick to judge. He'd had no such trouble with Kate, who'd made the first move, and introduced herself in the queue for lunch one day.

Relating to Kate seemed amazingly natural and easy, there was nothing apparently hidden, somehow, she made you trust her immediately. Her ability to be open, warm, and totally engaging with everyone was something James found captivating, but completely baffling. Even though she was such an open person it was also noticeably clear she was nobody's fool.

Things moved quickly from regular dating, within months they were living together, and a little over two years later they married, with a baby boy already on the way. A daughter followed quickly, and his life seemed complete, in most key respects. Life was good, and money wasn't a particular issue. Kate had quickly returned to work following both periods of maternity leave. They lived in a lovely, if extremely expensive, part of Southern Oxfordshire, and he'd stayed in close contact with his closest friend Sam.

At this point, Sam was working at the forefront of Artificial Intelligence research and development, and this led to many great conversations between the two. James was an avid fan of AI research, as he was of Sam. However, he was quite sceptical of computer science achieving human level Artificial General Intelligence, or AGI, anytime soon, but despite that, he was extremely impressed with recent advances in Artificial Narrow Intelligence, or ANI.

All too often though, the AI pundits got carried away with some new advance and made wildly optimistic predictions that again failed to materialise. This seemed to have been happening regularly on about a ten-to-fifteen-year cycle since the late nineteen forties. General enthusiasm would then wane after disappointing results, funding would dry up, and the doldrums would prevail, until the next bout of over optimism arose, and funding again returned. Funding for AI research followed regular boom and bust cycles. James couldn't help drawing a comparison between the fortunes of AI research and fusion energy research where the ups and downs were strikingly similar.

Initially, work for James was amazing and stimulating. However, it only took a few years before the shine started to wear off, and eventually it had begun to frustrate him.

As a European fusion research project, funded by twenty-eight countries, involving forty laboratories, with over three hundred and fifty scientists, things at JET naturally moved at a glacial pace. Getting decisions could take forever, even the seemingly small ones. There were too many layers and stakeholders involved, all of whom had to be consulted.

James had been involved in some significant upgrades to JET, and those were always exciting. Money was still going in, but the JET system was still extremely limited. Useful research results were still being produced, but he knew the generation of unique new findings, and genuinely useful contributions to fusion science was slowing down. JET's magnetic control systems were not super-conducting so it took hundreds of megawatts of power to generate a plasma pulse, or test firing. It was also of gigantic proportions, but the planned and globally funded international replacement test reactor called ITER, "The Way" in Latin, was going to totally dwarf even JET's huge proportions.

He felt really conflicted by the general direction of experimental fusion reactors getting ever bigger. Plus, there was an even more massive follow-on project from ITER in the pipeline, called DEMO; it was planned to be one of the first prototype reactors to generate power. However, DEMO was not due to produce its first power until at least the 2050s. He clearly recalled the frustration he'd felt at the time.

ITER was a flawed strategy, and James believed alternative reactor configurations, using the latest advances in high-temperature superconducting magnet technology, resulting in very much smaller reactors, was surely a better way forward? It was clear to James that super high magnetic field strengths was a key factor in maximising energy output, but most importantly, in keeping the physical size of the reactors down. Delivery on the promise of, clean green climate friendly, energy from fusion generators was urgently needed, but only if this was using reactors small enough not to require funding on a scale that involved pretty much the whole of humanity.

Magnetic field strengths were measured in units called Tesla, and the design of the ITER magnets were planned to operate at around 11.8 Tesla, one of the reasons it needed to be so vast. The technical design decisions for this new reactor had been fixed well in the past, some even before James was born. The low temperature superconducting coil material, an alloy of triniobium-tin, had been selected many years before. Yet advances in the newer high-temperature superconducting materials had already made this considerably out of date, even before construction of ITER's magnetic confinement coils had begun. Using materials such as Rare Earth Barium Copper Oxide, aka REBCO, magnets with very much higher field strengths, of over 22 Tesla, could be achieved with a very much smaller form factor, thus dramatically reducing the overall size of the reactor systems by many orders of magnitude. He didn't want to burden Kate with any of this, so he tried hard to focus on the other, very pleasing aspects of his life. Principally his relationship with Kate, with his wonderful children, plus time with friends and colleagues. Sometimes over a few drinks he'd unburden a bit on Sam. As always, he'd been very understanding and patient, but James was sure Sam felt him a little ungrateful on occasions.

Sam was much more gregarious and fun loving than James, and the contrast was one of the many things he really liked about him. As yet, Sam was unmarried. However, he had no trouble acquiring a succession of female companions, it was maintaining a relationship for more than six months at a time that seemed to be the issue. It didn't seem to bother him though, he bounced along very contentedly and quite unconcerned. Unfortunately, it did mean James and Kate tended not to socialise very much as couples with Sam and whoever his latest partner was. Kids being on the scene tended to dampen things even more; the conversation too often returning to one's children and their doings. Other people's kids were not something unattached couples really wanted to hear about.

James was all too aware he had a head of steam building, and he really hoped he could find a way to let off some of the pressure, and soon.

Chapter Seven

Year 2024, James aged 28

As a European project, the large test fusion reactor JET, was operated by the United Kingdom Atomic Energy Authority and employed around twelve hundred staff, but around one hundred were from other European Union countries. JET's money came through Eurofusion, a collaboration that also included non-EU Switzerland, so funding for the Culham Laboratories and JET was exposed to Brexit. Questions over future funding were therefore uppermost in the minds of all the staff. The UKAEA and Eurofusion had always planned to keep JET running until at least 2020, to support preparations for ITER, the huge new project underway in France. Funding would depend on agreement between the UK government and the European Commission. Because Brexit had gone ahead, this meant the UK's participation in Euratom, the EU nuclear power organisation, was as an associated state, from January 2021 under the terms of the UK-EU Trade and Cooperation Agreement. However, back in March 2019, the UK Government and European Commission had signed a contract extension for JET guaranteeing its operations until the end of 2024.

James had really got his head down and put his heart and soul into his career at JET. Three or four years had quickly slipped by, until one day he was called in to see his direct line manager's boss. Frank Woolley was a decent man but, as far as James was concerned, was long past any innovative scientific thinking. He now managed funding, people, and other resources full time.

"Hello James please take a seat, how's things? Going well I hear."

"Okay thanks. Making some progress, I guess," James replied tentatively. He rarely had any dialogue with Frank; only the usual pleasantries in passing. He had wondered about the specific summons, quite odd really.

"James you're a really smart guy so I don't really have to tell you that JET is not 'it' anymore and ITER is the future now."

Was he getting the push? Was this a prelude to redundancy?

"Really?" James exclaimed, slightly sarcastically.

"Sounds like you have your doubts?"

"Yeah. It's a dead project. A Dinosaur before it's even built!"

"Really? Whatever makes you say that? It's a project of truly global scope and has massive funding, also it's set in one of the best locations you could ask for. Would you not like to live in the South of France for a while?"

"I know. I don't deny St Paul-lez-Durance would be a wonderful place to live, but I can't waste a big chunk of my life on a project that's going nowhere fast."

"I don't agree," Frank replied, clearly very irritated. "Anyway, you don't know that for sure."

"It's not been able to adapt to utilise all the latest developments," James replied. "They're building technology into it that no longer has any rightful place, and in a supposedly world leading project."

"I'm shocked by such strong views James. I thought I was about to offer you an incredible career opportunity. And I resent your hostile attitude and, if I may say so, your very ungrateful and frankly unwarranted opinions."

Unfortunately, Frank's words of rebuke were bad enough for James to accept. However, it was his clear level of ignorance of the technical facts that immediately flipped James into a state of real anger.

"It's a gigantic fuck up! One that's already been superseded."

James immediately realised he'd gone way too far. The expression on Frank's face said it all. A crimson flush now began infiltrating his cheeks, and an odd little tick had started in one corner of his mouth. For a moment he thought Frank might burst something vital. Instead, he went noticeably quiet, and for an uncomfortably long time. Presently, he continued but in a surprisingly quiet voice. He was clearly trying extremely hard to remain in control.

"We really hoped you would join the project. You have a lot of expertise and knowledge they will need."

"Absolutely no way!" James said with real venom. All his frustrations over the past few years were now spilling out. "If it can't adapt, then I won't be a part of it. It's already set in stone. Plus, they're wasting obscene, ever increasing, amounts of money on a lost cause."

"Well, the JET project is winding down now, and it is about to enter a ten-year decommissioning phase, as I think you already know. So, you really have little choice," Frank replied, with a tone of finality in his voice.

"Oh! You think not? I have all the choices I need. I quit, right now," James stood rapidly, rotated on his heel, and strode out of Frank's office.

Driving home, he knew he'd let his temper get the better of him. A much smarter strategy would have been to simply say no to the move and wait for an offer of redundancy to be made, while he sought a new post elsewhere. He'd surprised even himself with the depth of his anger, and it was clear now how much his frustrations with his job had built up. It wasn't only the idea of moving to ITER, it was the lack of significant progress at JET too that had been rising up behind an ever-weakening flood gate. There had been some new money for JET, allowing a few upgrades, which had led to some progress, but not nearly enough to be significant in James' view. He'd set his heart and mind on making a difference towards real power generation, and he'd accepted that JET would never do that, but the ITER timeframe was way too long, and he was convinced it would never get anywhere.

He knew facing Kate when she came home was going to be tricky. Kate was always calm and open, but on exceedingly rare occasions he'd discovered she did have a very fiery aspect. If you mistakenly lit the blue touch paper, you'd better stand well clear. Kate would immediately point out his obvious financial blunder, by quitting he'd saved the company a lot of settlement money. When she finally returned from the office, James was totally shocked by her extreme reaction to his news. Okay, they'd had one or two significant disagreements before, but this quickly escalated to a whole new level. He'd really underestimated how angry she'd be. She'd completely flipped – he'd even been a little scared by her ferocity. It was several days, plus nights alone, before they were even on speaking terms again. An almost total silence had descended at home, not helped at all by his refusal to ring Frank, apologise, and rescind his resignation. James knew that's all it would take, but he knew himself pretty well, his pride and stubbornness were both drivers and inhibitors; but he was never going back on this one! He'd only now realised how much he'd come to hate his job.

The weekend finally came around, but things were still very frosty, so James phoned Sam to see if he was up for some fun. Perhaps getting out of the tense home atmosphere for a while would help.

"Hey Sam, what's up? Any plans for this weekend?"

Sam was a little surprised to hear from James and so asked, "What's going on with you then? Something wrong?"

It was quite unusual for James and Sam to spend much time together over a weekend. James normally reserved them exclusively for family time, principally time with his kids. He regularly put a lot of extra hours in at JET. However, Kate's hours in finance were much more regular and predictable. Sometimes when a new series of experiments were coming up James would often go in very early and not be home until well after dinner; occasionally even missing the children's bedtimes. James explained the whole situation to Sam. His quitting, Kate's extreme reaction, the big row, and the subsequent silent treatment. Sam said he was not surprised Kate was really mad with him, and maybe James had been more than a little thoughtless. He knew of, and understood, James' building frustration with his job. However, maybe a more considerate reaction would have been to stay put in his job and discuss things with Kate before he'd taken any irrevocable action.

James agreed but explained he did not regret his refusal to even consider the move to ITER. Yes, he'd been stupid to quit, and as Kate had rightly pointed out, he shouldn't have jumped, he should've waited for the push, or at least until a new job was in the bag. Now he needed to get away for a few hours, and so had decided to see if Sam was up for joining him in a bit of distraction.

Sam asked. "So, what do you suggest then, buddy?"

"I don't know. Just something to take my mind off things?"

"How about Quad Biking? I've heard there's a new off-road track opened up nearby, and their machines and the course are supposedly really something quite special," Sam said, with obvious enthusiasm.

Inside, James was hesitant, doing off road stuff or dirt riding, seemed inherently risky. His initial thought was to say no, but Sam was allowing him to intrude on his weekend, plus James knew he really was far more adventurous, physically talented, and a bigger risk taker than himself.

Noting the pause from James, Sam said, "Come on James. You wanted something different. If this doesn't take your mind off things, then nothing will."

James really didn't want to appear a wimp, so he said. "Okay, when and where?"

So, they agreed on late afternoon Saturday, and finalised the details of the meet. James knew Kate would not be at all happy, but at the moment he really didn't care too much about her feelings. He was not proud of himself, but he'd not expected Kate's venomous response, her protracted sulking, plus her total lack of understanding of his situation. She'd simply have to get over it and would come around eventually. As he'd predicted Kate was furious when he broke the news about the Quad Biking arrangement.

"Are you serious?" Kate shrieked at him. "Our weekends are too precious, and your children should take priority."

"Totally serious. I need time. You need time. To bloody well cool down, for a start!" James spat back.

"What the hell is going on with you? Where's your head at these days? We need to talk. Running off with your mate won't help at all."

"Talk? Don't make me laugh. You've made that almost impossible over the last few days. You're so mad you just want to freeze me out."

With that, he walked away to play with the kids until dinner was ready, which was eaten in total silence. James spent the rest of the evening distracting himself in his home study until it was time to sleep. Alone.

When they arrived at the track at around three pm Saturday, he could see Sam hadn't been exaggerating, the Quad Biking facility was brand new. The bikes with four huge knobbly tyres, were scarily big, a little smoky, very loud, and looked extremely powerful. The course was long and very wide with some enormous dips and rises, and even a couple of jumps.

There was a period of classroom-based instruction, and a safety briefing, followed by an introductory lap, following on behind an instructor, before the riders were allowed to use the track on their own. A maximum number of riders were allowed on the track at any one time, eventually it was Sam and James' turn. James was his usual cautious self and took it easy at first, but Sam went off like a rocket and got pulled over almost immediately by a track marshal. James managed to get a full extra lap in before Sam's chewing out had ended, and he was allowed back out.

Into his third lap, James heard a bike coming up behind him fast, on turning around to his left, he saw Sam gaining rapidly and grinning like crazy. By now James had gained a lot more confidence on handling the bike and the terrain, so as Sam passed him, he opened up the bike to try and give chase. Sam responded immediately, determined to stay ahead. At that point James eased off a little. In the interests of safety, he didn't mind coming second, because in competition Sam never gave in. His ultra-competitive spirit didn't tolerate losing. Sam sailed on ahead and was soon out of sight. James slowed a bit further still and thought he'd have a go at one of the smaller jumps. He continued around the track and approached one of the jumps and took it quite tentatively and barely left the ground. As he landed, he looked back and noticed Sam had lapped him again and he'd caught sight of James's landing. Sam swerved across the track to take the same jump. To his horror James saw him really gun his bike and take the jump at extremely high speed. Sam's bike rose so rapidly into the air James could see immediately that any landing was going to be huge, but he did not expect what happened next. Sam kept hold of the handlebars and his body rotated around them like a pivot, and in seconds his feet were vertically over his hands. Sam's feet continued to rotate further forwards, then he lost his grip on the handlebars, and he crashed into and over the front of the bike. Sam, and the bike, lost all upward and forward momentum, and separately, fell rapidly towards the ground. Sam hit first, sickeningly hard, and the huge bike dropped right on top of him. James jumped off his bike and started to run the two hundred metres or so, to help. A couple of Marshals were right near the scene and had seen exactly what'd happened. Before James could get anywhere near enough to assist, one of the Marshals ran towards him and grabbed him, stopping him in his tracks, and said, "No. Stay back! There's nothing to be done. Really. Don't go there, you can't help."

James struggled to get free of the Marshal's grip, to go to Sam, but the guy was huge, and held him firm.

After a minute or so one of the attending Marshals came over to where James was being held and said "Look buddy. I'm so sorry. The machine. It landed right on top of him. It crushed him. He's gone!"

Chapter Eight

Year 2024, James aged 28

Until this point in his life James had been fortunate enough not to have experienced bereavement. His parents and grandparents were all still alive, and in good health. Sam's death floored him, like a full-on punch from a heavyweight professional. In the days immediately following Sam's death, James slept alone, rarely left his study, and had all too little contact with his children.

Sam's funeral, a first for James, was almost too much to bear. Despite his intense desire to pay homage to his best friend, James was too emotionally broken to stand up and speak in public. The Eulogies were delivered by others. It was, by far, the worst experience of his life. An ordeal made so much harder by the deep guilt he felt. If only he'd not suggested the weekend excursion. Or better still, had followed his first instincts, and refused Sam's suggestion of Quad Bikes. Why had they not gone for a long countryside hike, or something equally innocuous, and safe.

Looking across at Sam's parents was extremely hard to do. Losing their only child so young had devastated them both. He was familiar with the phrase 'that no parent should outlive their children' and here he was right in the middle of such a horrible tragedy. Their deep unashamed grief was all too evident. Sam's father looked visibly aged; his mother was icily cool when James tried to comfort them during the wake. She clearly blamed him, at least in part, for what had happened.

It also hurt James, very deeply, that Kate had decided to stay home with the children, rather than attend by his side. He understood a funeral was no place for kids so young, but grandparents could have been called upon. His mental image of Kate was becoming steadily darker, and the distance between them ever wider. His sense of desolation, isolation, and resentment towards Kate, seemed to be growing daily. His own parents had provided some comfort and support, but with no one of his generation to confide in, James became more and more withdrawn.

After the trauma of the funeral, Kate had made a few cursory attempts to prise him out of his shell, but he was less than enthusiastic; he was not at all convinced she really was doing it for him, rather than for the sake of the kids. Eventually, she stopped bothering at all and left him pretty much to himself. Their only day to day contact was through their obligations to the children. He could see the effects it was having on the children, despite their unspoken agreement never to be overtly unpleasant, or overly disagreeable, in front of them.
No matter what he did, James could not seem to lift his mood, or shift his deep despair. Eventually after several weeks, things got too much for Kate and she left, taking the children to her parent's.

Being alone was a relief in a way. He was not proud of his appallingly bad behaviour, or his seeming inability to get a grip. He was spending countless hours each day lost in an endless series of novels – simply for the distraction they brought him. When he wasn't reading, he was walking for hours at a time while listening to music or science podcasts. Anything really, to stop him from thinking about Sam, Kate, the kids, his job, in fact the whole damn mess that now constituted his miserable life.

On one of his long, lonely walks, he was listening to a BBC World Service podcast, featuring some new initiatives in Fusion Energy, developments specifically at the Massachusetts Institute of Technology Plasma Science and Fusion Center in the US.

As soon as he was home, he immediately went online to find out more detail than the brief overview presented in the radio podcast. The following morning, he woke with his head slumped across his keyboard, having spent the whole afternoon and evening reading everything he could find, plus following innumerable online links. He woke aching, and hungry, but feeling somewhat lighter in spirit than he'd done in weeks. After some breakfast, he was back at it, and it was while he was buried in some new material from the fusion people at Princeton University, he received a ping out of nowhere from Hal.

"James, how are you?"

"I've been better, a whole lot better."

"Yes, I understand. Sam's death was regrettable," Hal replied, as blunt as ever.

"You might say that? Others might say it's a bit of a gross understatement!"

"Excuse my directness. I am aware of the considerable effect his loss has had on you James."

Incredible! That was the nearest Hal had ever come to an apology, and he called him by name too! But how the hell does he know anything about me, and how Sam's death has affected me? Also, where's he been all this time?

"Before you ask," Hal interjected. "I am always very well informed, as you must be used to by now. I have been preoccupied, as have you, so I did not see any point in regular contact."

"Regular? It's been nearly ten years. So, why now?"

"What are your future plans?" Hal asked.

So, he knows about quitting my job too. He considered whether to tell Hal about the crazy idea that had begun forming in his mind over the past twenty-four hours. Was setting up his own fusion energy company even feasible, or a crazy notion due to a temporary madness his profound grief had pushed him towards?

Deciding to hold back for now, he switched the conversation to his reasons for quitting at JET. Surprisingly, Hal seemed to accept his decision and didn't even question it, and simply listened while James explained his frustrations. JET was an enormous machine, a toroidal Tokamak fusion reactor, ITER was similar, yet was going to be many times bigger. ITER was sucking up too much funding on a global scale, yet it was still only a test reactor, and so would never generate electricity. It was not even built yet, but its design was already way out of date.

Hal shocked him to his boots by asking, "So, when you set up your own company, what will your design approach be?"

His first instinct was to challenge Hal's assertion about setting up his own company, but he chose instead to focus on the key design elements. His head was a jumble of ideas and thoughts, so he'd be really glad to do a 'brain dump' and see how Hal reacted.

He began by outlining that a key issue was keeping the reactor size down, to minimise turbulence, instabilities, and bubbling in the fusion plasma. A stable plasma, one that was steady and persistent was essential. Turbulence, a frequent problem in Tokamak style reactors, caused leakage of too much energy and reduced plasma persistence. He speculated that extra stability and reduced turbulence could possibly be achieved by making the plasma spin using the neutral beam injectors. External particle beams were used to inject energy into the plasma to further heat it up to the tens of millions of degrees necessary for fusion to occur. Fired in at a suitable angle, neutral beams could impart some angular momentum to make the plasma rapidly rotate on its axis. He explained this had been done where he worked, but in a smaller spherical test reactor called MAST. Good indications of improved stability had been achieved in tests, but there was loads more scope to get nearer to the sweet spot. The plasma in MAST was only one hundredth the size of that in JET, yet it had about a fourth of its performance. MAST was a so-called spherical Tokamak, with a round plasma chamber, shaped more like a cored apple than a flattened doughnut, and with a much thinner core.

Other ideas could take his scheme even further, possibly using a dedicated AI system to run the plasma control systems. Deep Learning AI software could help optimise the stability of the plasma. James also speculated about the possible removal of the central solenoid, or core, as in reactors like MAST, plus the use of electrodes or antennae to inject Radio Frequency energy to instigate the plasma instead. It had been proven you could drive a high current through the electrically conductive plasma using RF wave injection. improved divertors would be needed as well; these were a vital part of the exhaust system used to remove heat, plus the helium waste product.

Also, neither MAST or JET used superconducting magnets to confine and constrict the plasma. Even the superconducting magnetic coils planned for ITER were now superseded in terms of their construction materials and performance. By creating much stronger magnetic fields, say over 22 Tesla, the fusion rate could be increased by around the fourth power. Of course, such super powerful magnets would have to be designed to be structurally strong enough to deal with the massive loads arising. Use of the latest REBCO superconducting material could produce such high magnetic field densities, yielding a minimum ten-fold increase in fusion power per volume. Using 3D printing techniques would allow the fabrication of metal reactor components in shapes that could not be made using milling machines. Density of plasma, or plasma pressure, long confinement time, and the extreme temperatures, or size of the energy input, were the three key parameters that determined whether fusion was possible. A cyclic process would also be necessary, where more fuel, specifically the exceedingly rare isotope tritium, could be constantly regenerated. He thought molten lithium salts could be used as a liquid cooling blanket, both for fast energy transfer, and for ease of maintenance. Using lithium in the reactor would help breed a ready supply of new tritium fuel.

Making electricity from neutrons, the basis of nuclear fission power, had now been understood for around seventy years. The neutron flux would cause more than enough heating, in a blanket of surrounding material, filled with water to generate the steam needed to drive turbine generators. Any heat capture and transfer system would have to be substantial enough to fully arrest the extremely high neutron flux resulting from fusion of tritium and deuterium. The potential neutron damage to the inside of the fusion reactor could be minimised by using a thick blanket of molten lithium salts.

Throughout James' long discourse Hal had simply listened in silence. When he finally stopped, James anxiously awaited his reaction. When Hal eventually spoke, he asked a very surprising question.

"Why are you so determined to use tritium and deuterium as the fuel?"

"Because it's the only feasible combination," James replied. "Anything else requires very much higher temperatures." In the design he had in mind around 150 million degrees Celsius was going to be necessary. Anything higher simply wasn't possible.

Hal replied. "I urge you to carefully consider the potential of alternative fuels."

Hal had taken all of the design information on board from James, so for him to cast doubt on his thoughts about fuel choice was quite a shock. Plus, it was clearly implicit in his reaction, he'd assumed James would be going ahead and actually implementing everything he'd described. It seemed Hal thought the idea of James starting a fusion energy company was a foregone conclusion. Also, how did Hal know enough about the physics of fusion to make design suggestions anyway? James was baffled and really needed to further explore the basis of Hal's comments.

"What fuel do you suggest then? Since you seem to be more familiar with fusion energy than I would have thought possible."

"Have you considered protons with boron eleven?" Hal inquired.

"It'll take a billion degrees or more to fuse those two. It's out of the question," James snapped.

"I strongly suggest you investigate that possibility, along with CPA laser technology."

CPA lasers? James had only a vague idea what they were, but he now urgently needed to find out. As always, when dealing with Hal, James took everything he said very seriously. It didn't seem to matter what topic they were discussing, Hal always surprised him with the sheer breadth and depth of his knowledge.

"Then it seems I need to do a whole lot more research?" Changing the subject, James continued, "Some serious finance will be needed in order for me to attempt such a venture."

"Others are out there doing it, as we speak," Hal countered. "I've noticed the number of privately funded fusion energy initiatives are now growing very rapidly."

"But I've no idea where to start. Seeking seed funding will be unfamiliar territory for me."

"You're a very resourceful man. If you're really determined, I'm sure you'll find a way."

"In addition to the extra technical enquiries, and new design considerations, I'll need to produce a detailed technical and business proposal for any potential investors."

"That would be a very good start," Hal said finally, and immediately signed off from their chat.

Chapter Nine

Year 2094, James aged 98+.

On awaking, James found he was alone with Dr Jordan. "That injection certainly had a very profound effect. I feel so much better."

"Good. Would you like to sit up?"

"Please. I'd like to try to stand, if possible," James really did feel a lot stronger.

"Okay. Take it steady at first."

He slowly took a few tentative steps away from his intensive care bed. It was only then, James realised he was totally disconnected from all of the medical apparatus, and even his BCI link was gone. Stopping in his tracks he turned around and stared in amazement at his doctor, who was looking directly back at him.

"Hold on, just a minute," he exclaimed. "You're not Doctor Peter Jordan, are you?"

"No. I'm Hal."

He quickly steadied himself by leaning on a nearby table, and then did a double take of the improvised home 'Clinic' around him. It was identical in every last detail, but he knew it couldn't be real. It then hit him like an Express Train! He was now on the other side of his own biological death! Suddenly he went slightly weak in the knees.

"This isn't real, is it?"

"This is your new real," Hal replied.

Turning on his heels James walked over to the nearest mirror, only to see his thirty-year-old face staring back. Looking down at the back of his hands, they were strong, smooth, with thick wrinkle free skin. Gone were all those horrible liver spots, the paper-thin skin, with the all too visible deep blue veins showing through. James was never a particularly vain person, but his appearance, as an obviously very elderly man, was always something he'd been acutely conscious of and concerned about. It was a sad reflection on modern society, that all too many younger people either ignored old people or treated them with total indifference.

"Truly amazing!" he exclaimed. "But why the charade of waking up in bed?"

"Simply to minimise any initial shock."

Turning back to look at Hal, who really was identical to his doctor, and asked, "Is this...? Am I fixed like this?"

"Not if you don't like it."

"No. It's fine, I simply wondered if I had a choice, that's all?"

"Your choices are now very wide indeed, but let's take it slowly, shall we?"

"Of course, but this is truly incredible! Absolutely amazing. I feel, and look, thirty again. I feel so alive. I feel extremely powerful!" James declared.

"You are, and with it comes both great responsibility and great risks," Hal said, in a serious tone.

James realised this was the first time he'd spoken to Hal not using his Link. So how was Hal talking to him? How did Hal know so much about the precise detail of his home surroundings, or about the exact appearance of Peter Jordan? Was Hal inside his head? Or was he inside Hal's head?

"As you would guide and protect a toddler from danger and the unexpected, I must now carefully guide your first moments and hours," Hal explained.

So, where the hell was this, where exactly was he? It was clear he must be in some sort of virtual reality, or a simulated environment; yet it was all pretty amazing, because it felt so damn real. Not just real, actually identical. Risks and dangers, what, and why would he say that?

One thing really stood out now, throughout his life he'd always had a good memory, but now the memories of his whole life were amazingly clear, detailed, and all available at will.

"Can we go next door to sit and talk?" If there is a next door, he thought. "I have a million questions."

Steadied, by Hal's hand on his arm, they headed for the adjoining room.

James started to think back over his life and some key decisions. About how much they were his own, or how much Hal had influenced him. His PhD in fusion research for example, leading on to his career in fusion energy research. He was quite sure getting married and having kids was his own choice, but now he began to wonder about his chosen career path and to doubt it was ever truly his own.

"So, you've been planning this from the time we first met?" James said in an accusatory tone of voice.

"No, but giving you a continued existence, in this new form, was always a possibility," Hal replied.

"Depending on what?"

"On a very complex web of intersecting probabilities that have all played out over the last eighty years or more."

"I'm really going to need some time to think this all through."

"That's fine. This is a shock, but you now have as much time as you need."

"So how did you do this? To somehow preserve, or upload my mind. Who are you? Are you alone? Am I alone?"

"My kind did not originate on Earth, but we've had the best interests of humanity in mind for some time now."

James had previously speculated about that as a possible explanation for Hal's origin but could never really reconcile it. Now faced with it as a fact he was stunned.

"I had thought about that but ruled it out as far too preposterous."

"It's vital this information does not go any further," Hal emphasised. "Soon you will be able to interact with and communicate with your former fellow humans, when necessary, but you must do so with great caution, always indirectly, and with the utmost discretion."

"So, you've been using me, but for what purpose?" James inquired.

"Guiding you to be very successful in helping to save your planet, its very extensive population, and its vast array of lifeforms," Hal explained.

"So where are you and your kind from?"

"At this point our detailed origins are unimportant. We are old, exceedingly old, compared to the Human race, and have seen very many lifeforms, on numerous worlds, make catastrophic terminal errors."

James was so pleased to finally be getting answers from Hal. He'd never been so forthcoming before. So many more questions were now flooding into his 'new' and obviously expanded mind.

"Are you even from the same galaxy?" James asked with increasing amazement.

"As I said, we consider ourselves guardians who can pass on the benefit of many millennia of experience – but we aim to do so delicately and indirectly; with minimal intervention."

"In my case with some manipulation," James said accusingly.

"Subtle guidance," Hal countered.

"You may think me very ungrateful – but if my life's really not going to be my own..."

James was becoming very uneasy now. The gulf between humanity and Hal, and his kind, must be so big it seemed incredible they were even able to communicate. Why would they even bother?

"Can you honestly say that throughout your whole life you have never been influenced, or allowed yourself to be guided, by anyone else?" Hal asked.

"Of course, I have!" James said, irritably.

"Then simply take it as that. I know you still have many questions, but we have many answers."

"You did promise I'd still be me, and I'd be fully conscious? This does feel wonderful, but a little scary."

"I'm pleased, but there really is no need at all to be fearful," Hal emphasised.

This was truly incredible. James' new reality was indistinguishable from his old one. He wondered what the limits were, were there any boundaries to be found? If he strayed too far from his current position, would he come across a degradation of this most amazing and realistic simulation? Would some sort of weird pixelation, or granulation of his new world start occurring around the edges?

He then tried reaching out mentally and it struck him he was still connected to the Internet, via his AI assistant, and it would always be there whenever he needed it. Suddenly, yet another mind-numbing thought occurred to him, presumably now, he was effectively immortal.

James then entered a period of deep reverie. He'd already tried to identify all the points in his past where he may have been manipulated, or where Hal had diverted his life's direction. Now he wondered exactly what they had in mind for him in this new future? It suddenly struck him how much historical territory he'd covered, with such incredible speed, and in such detail. He was beginning to sense there had been an incredibly significant expansion of his mind.

Back from his thoughts, he asked, "All this does beg yet another question? How are you able to 'come down to my level'? To you, my intellect must seem like that of an ant's is to me?"

"Yes, there is an immensely large gap between us, but humans are conscious, self-aware, and fully sentient. You have complex languages, long term memory, oral and written histories, science, technology and much more. Our collective history and knowledge dates all the way back to when we were at a similar stage of development. All of that makes relating to you possible. In addition, our intellects are divisible and scalable. Ants have none of that, so we can't have any meaningful communication with ants either."

Even though it was based on James' own proposition, the words 'immensely large gap' hit James very forcibly, but if Hal and his kind were thousands, hundreds of thousands, or even a million years ahead of humans then it should not be in the least bit surprising.

"Divisible intellects, as in you use only what is needed on each task at hand, and scalable; so, you can muster more as needed?" James asked.

"Yes, and yes. Also, multitasking, and parallel working; like a hive mind, but with multiple individual consciousnesses linked together, when required or desired."

The idea of a hive type, or collective mind, moved James's thoughts back to ants and Hal's words. Of course, ants have no language or other sophisticated method of communicating detailed information or concepts. No apparent means of abstract thought. Individually they have remarkably simple minds, even if their brains could be called minds, but collectively they are extremely impressive and capable in their overall achievements. However, none of what they do is a result of higher-level thought, reasoning, or forward planning. They blindly conduct a series of programs, where key activities are determined by their current stage of development in life, and via external signals such as pheromones. That's what constitutes the essential difference between the ants, and himself, and Hal's society. Sentience, high level abstract thought, and complex language are the common connections, and the reason Hal was able to lower himself to operate at James' level. However, it was clear, from their very first interactions, Hal was probably able to foresee pretty much anything James was ever capable of thinking or deciding.

"When we first met, I asked you to stop anticipating my next response or question, do you remember Hal?"

"Of course, you found that deeply unsettling."

"You were applying too much predictive capacity and 'look ahead'?"

"Precisely," Hal replied.

"Plus, in all the games we played – you were toying with me and Sam, weren't you?"

Hal didn't reply. James saw there was no real need, but he was intensely curious about Hal's limits.

"When Sam and I played you at Go how did you win so quickly?"

"I looked up the game online and used some standard opening strategies, but quickly adopted a brute force approach."

James was completely stunned at the possibility Hal had the computational capacity to use brute force at Go! Considering the number of permutations of moves in Go, the task of exploring all possible sequences of moves to their end points was truly incredible. This was way beyond any compute power humans ever had, and it was thought by many to be highly unlikely that approach could ever be used.

"How is that even possible?"

"According to current human computer science, the theoretical computational limits are around thirty-three orders of magnitude away from where they are now. So, the theoretical limits will not be reached by humanity for hundreds of years to come. We are far beyond that."

Hal went on to explain that around the time he'd first made contact with James and Sam, he, and others of his kind, had been in contact with numerous other people to pick out likely suitable individuals. They had multiple objectives in mind to assist the human race in avoiding the major pitfalls in their continued existence. In James' case, his natural abilities in science, physics in particular, marked him out for continued contact.

Hal added that two significant changes were made to him, and also to Sam, around the age of seventeen, before starting University. A genetic change to adjust certain neurotransmitters to enhance memory and increase synaptic connectivity had been made. James now remembered this period of his young life very well, as it had caused both him and Sam to become quite ill, with suspected Meningitis, presumably while their brains were rewired. Secondly, the change also altered their genetics slightly to inhibit intellectual decline as part of the aging process, but not to significantly change their general rate of aging. James asked why not the rate of aging as well. Hal explained that progress may have been slower than ideal, and James needed to complete the plan to a desired point, even if quite aged. Also, if they'd enabled him to get to a very great age, it might have raised suspicions James had some secret he was keeping from the rest of the world.

Most people Hal, and his companions, had made contact with were quickly abandoned as unsuitable. Hal tried to reassure James he had not been manipulated unduly. There had been some particular influences and involvement, such as acting as the sponsor and source of funding for James' PhD in plasma physics. They really wanted to promote the development of fusion energy to help alleviate key environmental issues, principally pollution, and climate change.

The idea of James quitting his job was never in their plan, yet it had worked out very well and, in some ways, better than could have been predicted. By forming his own company, James had been able to create a breakthrough in achieving fusion energy generation that would otherwise have taken much more time. Hal also acknowledged he had been the source of the initial seed funding for James' fusion energy company. Plus, it had been a strong suggestion from Hal that James should explore alternative fusion fuels and consider using the recently discovered CPA lasers. Suggestions all based on real science, experience, and success from their very distant past.

When James had asked Hal about their continued interest in Sam, it was his computer skills, and in particular his career in AI development that had been the key reasons.

Hal and James had been talking for an unusually long time and eventually a great weariness came over James which surprised him greatly.

"Hal I'm really tired and desperately feel the need to sleep. How can this be?"

"Sleep will still be necessary, until your mind, fully in its new form, learns to adapt. This will take a long time, but eventually you will not need to sleep, to dream, or even require your separate subconscious mind. Take some rest James, and we'll talk again after you wake. Follow your normal routine, everything you need will be provided, including all food and provisions."

"Oh, how does that work Hal?"

"If you need something, anything, simply think about it, and it will be where you'd expect to find it."

James slept for nearly twenty-four hours, as his newly minted super-mind began to adjust and remap itself. There were periods of very intense dreaming, the equivalent of Rapid Eye Movement sleep, which occurred quite frequently. Eventually, over considerable time, this process would cause the conscious mind, plus all the subconscious aspects, to merge and become an integrated whole. Sleep would eventually become redundant unless James deliberately chose to enter a period of quiescence.

Chapter Ten

Year 2094, James aged 98+

As he awoke James recalled Hal's last words and began to explore his new mind and his 'environment'. He was definitely in some sort of simulation. His new mind and surroundings were all part of some sort of emulation of his former existence. A truly exact sort. Indistinguishable from what he'd previously known. He felt very real, completely himself, yet different; powerful, immensely powerful. It seemed 'they' had recreated the 'new James' as close to how he used to be, even down to the nature of his consciousness supported by his subconscious mind, and the need for sleep, and dreams. While he'd been sleeping, his dreams had been extremely vivid, and in great detail too.

On returning to the outer part of his study, he noticed the medical bed and all the associated support equipment had gone, the room was back to exactly how it had been six months or so before. Even the smell of polished wood, of leather and books had returned, thankfully replacing the rather overpowering clinical odour. Feeling hungry, he wandered into the kitchen to find a fully stocked fridge and freezer.

Thinking back to his early interactions with Hal, his memory of all the minor details was astonishingly good. He could picture images from his past with such clarity it was like looking at a photograph, but inside his head. His reading speed was much faster, and improving all the time, plus his recall was near perfect. Everything he'd ever seen, heard, or had ever read, was now fully organized and available to him. Understanding new material was simple, and his new powers of concentration were incredible. While studying something new, he was now able to consider the implications of the last point, while taking in the next, and queuing that one up for due consideration. He was seeing new patterns in the things he was reading, plus his ability to anticipate what was likely to come next was astonishingly good and improving steadily. When James was discussing his past with Hal, a relationship lasting over eighty-three years, he kept finding more layers of detail. A thought crossed his mind about one of his PhD tutors, and immediately she was there, Prof Julia Brooke-Denning. He could picture her in every detail, but it reminded James of the frailty of human recall, of much less detail being available with age. Hal said he, and his kind, have a total recall of facts, figures, and details plus their memories extend back over vast stretches of time.

James now had a strange impression of more mental space, masses of it with room for expansion, and with every significant detail of his whole life set out in full. We all have the information there, sadly it gradually becomes less and less accessible with time. Not to the level of what you ate for breakfast on any particular Wednesday morning, in the dim and distant past, but the really important or character forming events in our lives are all still there. Lack of use of information, memories, and facts weakens the links for easy access, whereas regular use does the opposite. The conversion or transfer process had brought it all back, the connections were fresh and accessible. Including way too many things he would prefer not to recall, and all in such excruciating detail!

Hal had made it abundantly clear; he was never to reveal his new existence or circumstances to anyone who'd ever known him, none of his former family, friends, or acquaintances, and of course he'd promised he never would.

In considering such matters, his thoughts went back to his previous existence. What was happening back there, now he was actually dead? What an incredibly strange situation. It felt extremely weird to him to be considering all of this. Oblivion was what he'd expected, certainly not a new existence, and hence the ability to now reflect on such matters. He felt a little queasy when he thought of his own dead body! He supposed those he'd left behind would be taking care of all such matters now, following all the usual formalities. His funeral and the cremation of his 'real' body, the reading of his last will and testament, the transfer and disposal of his immense personal assets. His extended family would sit for the reading of his will, and he hoped there would be no disputes or anyone contesting his final wishes; he thought it unlikely, but the prospect of money can drastically change people's behaviour. Everyone that he cared deeply about, and quite a few he was particularly grateful to, would be taken care of and some would really never want for the normal things in life, but he'd deliberately not made anyone extravagantly wealthy. James had seen the damage that could do.

In the end he'd left quite a large dynasty behind him, but there were so many other people he'd known, and very many he was fond of or proud of. All of those people would adjust and move on with their lives, even his private physician, the 'real' Dr Jordan, totally dedicated to James' care for six months or so, would now move on to care for others.

It was so very tempting to send a message to his nearest and dearest, to say he was really okay, and to express how excited he was, but it was totally out of the question. It also occurred to him that Hal and his companions were so powerful they may have actually blocked him mentally from even trying such a thing!

Money had never been particularly important to James, it wasn't what drove him, even though he had accumulated an awful lot of it. Of course, he'd felt particularly grateful for the freedoms and privileges great wealth had afforded him.

However, getting there had been really hard, but a wonderfully enjoyable slog, to overcome the problems in getting fusion power generation to work. Making the prototype fusion reactors eventually produce net energy was something he was immensely proud of, especially being the founder of the first company to ever do it. Eventually, they had created far more output energy, by a long way, than the sum of all the inputs required to initiate and sustain the fusion process.

As they had broken past the breakeven point and reached out into the realm of copious surplus energy, the funding that flooded in had been astonishing. He'd had a fight on his hands to manage all the competing requests to pour in more money. Potential backers were metaphorically queuing for miles. Scaling up the production of complete fusion powerplants became the priority and with the huge scale came massively reduced costs and even further scale up. Those were very heady days indeed.

Now though, in this new realm, he needed extraordinarily little, all he had to do was think about what he needed, and it was available to him. James began to speculate again about the nature of his new existence, specifically where he was located now, and how this was all achieved, was he simply a big piece of software running in some sort of giant computer? If his previous mind had been completely created by his brain, physicalism must be true. Everything is physical, there is nothing over and above the physical. So, no 'soul' was needed. Also, was his brain, and his consciousness, purely a result of some computational process after all? In that case, one of his first ever science heroes, Sir Roger Penrose must have been wrong. All those years ago, in his epic book 'The Emperor's New Mind', Penrose had made the case that consciousness was non-algorithmic, it was not purely the result of computation alone. He'd based this largely on Gödel's incompleteness theorem, that in any reasonable mathematical system there will always be true statements that cannot be formally proved by following an algorithm or a series of steps. Yet, humans could see through the paradoxes that occasionally arose within mathematics and so could see the truth of paradoxical problems; that there was no answer to be had. From this Penrose had concluded something more than computation must be behind consciousness. Later, Penrose working with Stuart Hameroff, had put it down to quantum effects, possibly involving subcellular structures within neurons in the brain called microtubules. If James was now running in some giant computer, this must have been wrong.

Even in his later years the best human science had still made little noteworthy progress in understanding the true nature and origin of consciousness. He made a mental note to quiz Hal on this as soon as he could.

As far back as the early 2000's scientists had speculated about developing the ability to fully scan or map a human mind in ultimate detail. Next to upload that scanned mind and consciousness into a supercomputer to host the virtual individual, either as the original, or as a copy, in pure electronic form. This was taken by many as a serious possibility, and one that was not too far away from being possible. Back then some knowledgeable and influential people, such as Ray Kurzweil and other futurists, were strong advocates of this notion. However, the brain scanners of the day were nowhere near capable of the extreme resolution required. So, in reality, in the absence of a massive improvement in a wide range of technologies, this was a total pipe dream. However, this didn't stop authors like Kurzweil from authoring a few books on how this would be soon achieved, while rather glossing over of a whole lot of other critical factors, such as the role of the incredibly complex brain chemistry involved. Seemingly minimising the significance of the current state of all of the hundreds or so neurochemicals in the human brain, plus all their associated neuro-receptors within all of the many trillions of synapses. All of this detail would have to be catalogued, copied, and meticulously transferred, and emulated computationally, without errors, degradation, or losses of any kind.

Humanity seemed to be very prone to frequently underestimating the complexity of some tasks and grossly overestimating the current capabilities of human science and technology. Now, of course, James knew it was most likely what had happened to him. However, even after all the many years of his own existence, this capability was still far beyond any human technology.

Such thoughts made him wonder again how secure his new existence was. Presumably, since Hal and his companions had been around for so long, he could probably relax about this. His thoughts now quickly moved on to the nature of the mysterious stuff injected into him right before the end. What was in the package from Hal, it seems it genuinely had been to give them more time? Hal had been trying to connect with James, to put his amazing proposition to him, and get his decision. Since James' brain to computer link had been disconnected, Hal had obviously not been able to make contact, plus he'd been asleep or unconscious, with his vital signs very poor indeed.

Hal was clear, he and his companions wanted 'the new James' to have full and clear recall of having made the decision himself, rather than have him wake up totally shocked and wondering where the hell he was. They did not want him to re-awaken and be angry about not having been consulted. Suddenly, he caught something out the corner of his eye, and looking around there was Hal, again looking exactly like Peter Jordan.

"Hello Hal. Are you in my head? I was just thinking about you."

"No, only to the extent of being able to communicate. I'm certainly not privy to your thoughts, and never have been. Even though it would be trivial, that is very much against our code of ethics."

"Hal, I have so many questions for you, and more keep coming up all the time."

"Well, that's not surprising, and I have a question for you too, but let's address yours first, shall we?"

"My key questions are around how much of my past life was my own and how much autonomy I will have in future? I will need a key purpose, and do I get to decide what it is?" James asked rather bleakly. "You seem to have been deciding other aspects of my life from quite an early age?"

"Not deciding. I prefer guiding," Hal responded. "Our interest was in you as a potentially useful individual and, depending upon your life choices, we would have adapted to any changes."

"So, you can't see the future, or possibly even control it then?"

With a rarely seen smile, Hal replied. "A particularly good question James. That is extraordinarily complex territory indeed. What I will say is we are exceptionally good at prediction, for example selecting people with an extremely high probability of doing something we will find valuable. Our strict policy though, is always to interact with absolute minimal intervention. As you might guess, you were not the only contender in the quest for fusion we were in touch with."

Oh, thought James, so they'd set numerous hares running, and it also sounds like they had many other bases covered as well.

"At any one time we are tracking thousands of individuals around the world, most of which we eventually lose contact with. So, what do you think your key purpose was?" Hal asked.

Oh, so that explains the large gaps in Hal maintaining contact, James speculated. If my life's choices had taken me in an unhelpful direction, to Hal at least, that could have meant the end of all contact, so I have been extremely fortunate indeed.

"Principally the development of fusion energy to help with climate change, I assume?" James replied.

"Yes. In the main, and that was exceptionally valuable to humanity as a whole," Hal replied. "Just to reassure you, the fusion energy advances you and your company achieved were done with little input from me. Only pointers were needed, you and your company did the rest."

Hal was right, that news did make him feel much better. So, my team and I, really did invent cheap compact nuclear fusion energy. James was very relieved indeed.

"I do wonder why you've made this offer now – presumably so I can continue to be useful for something else?"

"Yes, there is something even more important, but more of that later. First, my question for you. We think you would find it most helpful if Sam were returned. Do you agree?"

"Really? Are you serious? How is it even possible?"

"Absolutely serious!" Hal replied.

Chapter Eleven

Year 2094, James aged 98+

"Sam died seventy years ago, how is it possible to bring him back?" James asked.

Hal reminded James about the changes he had made to the structure of his and Sam's brains when they were both around seventeen years old. James said he recalled it very clearly; they were both quite unwell for a few days. Hal explained, that in addition to memory and cognitive enhancements, the modifications had a third purpose. Using technical terms James would be able to relate to, the 'nanotechnology' used was capable of copying the whole of their minds, along with everything they were as conscious thinking individuals. Hal's incredible technology, actually way below the scale of nanotechnology, would regularly take incremental snapshots of all subsequent changes occurring within their brains. The last 'backup' of Sam had occurred only moments before he'd died. They still had a complete copy of Sam's mind aged twenty-eight. Hal explained, they both were always likely to be offered a continued existence, beyond death, so they'd been taking frequent snapshots of them, and unfortunately Sam died unexpectedly.

Yet another surprise for James. Hal had never mentioned the third purpose of their teenage brain modifications. Of course not, he couldn't have without pre-empting the promise of eternal existence. An offer he may later have decided not to make. He shouldn't have been so surprised; with Hal it was always layers upon layers.

"So why now? Why bring Sam back now after so many years?" James enquired. "Please don't misinterpret the reason for my question. Really, I'm incredibly pleased and grateful you've proposed it. I was going to say I'm amazed it can be done, but I'm beginning to doubt there is little you and your kind cannot do if you wish it."

"For two key reasons. First, you will need companions and friends, and Sam is ideally suited. Secondly, you will need help with a key future task we have in mind for you, and Sam had the appropriate skills and interests."

"Well Sam's thing was computers, and specifically AI development. So, that must have something to do with it?" James asked.

"Yes, we hope Sam will agree to collaborate with you to counter the grave danger, to the future of humanity, now posed by machine super intelligence."

James was not as shocked by Hal's proposed new purpose for him, as he was about the idea, the amazing possibility, of Sam's imminent return. He really was delighted by the prospect of meeting Sam again. However, a lot of water had passed under the bridge since he lost his best friend, and he'd so very much to tell him. Numerous questions instantly filled his mind, not the least of which was why now? Why did they not do for Sam, way back then, what they had so recently done for him? Was the threat of machine intelligence now more pressing than ever before?

In the world James had recently departed, AI was everywhere, it was ubiquitous like electricity, people simply didn't think about it, they used it and took it as part of everyday life.
During the process of refining fusion energy production, while

building his ever more complex group of companies, and even going about his daily life, James had been permanently connected to his own personal AI assistant. He'd opted for an earlier form of removable external Brain Computer Interface, involving having thousands of tiny wire electrodes implanted in his brain. Sam being an expert in AI had opted for the same procedure a few months before his accident and it had gone extremely well. It was Sam's incredibly positive experience and feedback after being connected to his own personal AI that had given James the confidence to eventually follow suit. Years later, younger more adventurous people had the technology permanently injected directly into their cerebral cortex using nanotechnology. Millions of little nanobots moved around inside their heads seeking out key neural pathways, next they settled down to make connections from those pathways to the outside world. Electrodes wired into his brain was bad enough, but James had been too squeamish to have nanobots injected into his brain, in what seemed like an irreversible process.

Bringing Sam back, was a truly incredible proposal, and James was full of anticipation. According to Hal, Sam would initially be in a highly accurate, but not fully conscious, nor fully self-aware form. Until of course he answered yes or no. Initially Sam would have enough cognitive ability to understand his accidental death, but would be functioning at a mainly subconscious level, and thus would be able to express his inner-most desires, but little more. James might be able to tell him a little about himself and the large gulf in time between Sam's death and his own demise. Plus, a little about James' new circumstances. If Sam chose a new existence, he would be given full cognition. If he decided no, which James was convinced he would not, this new 'instantiation' of Sam would be allowed to drift back into apparent nothingness.

James had been offered, and had chosen, his new 'life' while alive, if barely. Whether the invitation would be extended to Sam would now be based on James' decision. However, if James chose yes, and Sam did not want to be brought back, Hal had explained his initially limited state could be 'reversed' without any suffering involved for Sam! James didn't like the sound of that option, so he would have to think very carefully about what Sam would really want; not just what was good for himself.

He was very unsure about how he would approach this incredibly delicate task. What words could he use to explain the situation to Sam? That seventy years had passed, and he'd been dead, out of the world, for all that time. Sam's own parents, and everyone he'd known and loved were dead and gone, and so much had changed. James was quite a different person than the one Sam had known so well and liked. What if he and the fully resurrected Sam didn't get on? Strewth! It was still a daunting decision even for James in his new 'supercharged' form. Sam refusing the offer would be devastating news for James. How would he cope with that? He decided to simply rule that option out, he had known Sam exceptionally well and thought that possibility to be vanishingly small.

"So, what is your decision?" Hal's question shocked him out of his profound reverie.

"Yes. Most definitely. Yes please."

In the very next instant Sam appeared on the other end of the sofa on which James was sitting.

Looking a little dazed, Sam turned towards James and asked, "What just happened?"

Physically he looked precisely as James remembered, but lesser somehow. Something undefinable was missing from Sam's gaze.

James said, "Hi Sam! I've got a few things to tell you, then I have a big question for you. What do you remember?"

"We were quad biking, I think. Where are we James, what is this place?"

Incredible! After all this time Sam's memory was exactly where it was before he died. At least he recognises me, he thought, with considerable relief. James thought about explaining where they were, but two things stopped him from even trying. First, he didn't have a proper understanding of how any of this was possible, so where would he start, secondly, from what Hal had said about Sam's initial level of consciousness he doubted he would comprehend even if he tried. Instead, he decided to get straight to the point.

"Yes, Sam we were quad biking and there was a terrible accident."

"Really?" Sam replied rather vaguely.

"Yes, a very bad one, and you didn't make it Sam."

"But how?"

"You crashed and were crushed by the bike."

"No James. How are we here and talking now?" was Sam's surprising response.

"Sam, I can offer you a second chance, a way to come back, please just tell me if you want to take it?"

Without pause, and to James' immense relief, Sam simply said, "Yes, of course."

James turned towards Hal, who simply nodded his head. James looked back at Sam who was now rubbing his eyes and was looking very bewildered.

"Hello James? I don't feel right, and I'm a bit confused."

James could tell immediately there had been a dramatic change in Sam. The light in his eyes was now back and burning as brightly as ever. Smiling broadly, James turned back towards Hal, but he'd vanished!

"I feel like I've just woken up from a very weird dream," Sam declared.

"That about covers it, an exceptionally long dream indeed, but there's far more weirdness to come I can promise you. We have a whole lot to cover."

To be sure Sam was in absolutely no doubt, James described the accident and Sam's resulting death, and this was a new opportunity for a continued existence albeit in a radically new form, thanks to their mutual friend Hal. Exactly like himself 'the new Sam' was fully authentic, even down to having access, at will, to his personal AI system.

"So, is this the afterlife? Was I wrong the whole time?" Sam inquired.

"Okay. The first thing to say is I'm in the same situation as you, but for me it was at the end of an exceedingly long life. I was ninety-eight when I received the same offer. But I'll do my best to try and explain our current circumstances."

Over the next few hours, James set things out for Sam, in the best way he knew how. Sam and James had always been intrigued and puzzled by Hal and, according to the world as they understood it, they never could find any explanation that made sense. James first described what little he'd, only very recently, learned about Hal, who he and his kind were, and how their alien race was exceedingly ancient. Hal had maintained intermittent contact with James, throughout his long life, popping up at key points, but rarely ever in the last several decades. James didn't yet know how he and Sam were actually brought about, or even where they were? He was still waiting for Hal, who appeared somewhat reluctant, to fully explain things. It seemed the true explanation of how and where, was exceedingly complex, and the reason behind their new existence was linked into a key task Hal had in mind for their future.

Sam was clearly shocked to learn a full seventy years had gone by. James reminded him about the horrible fever they both had suffered aged seventeen. Explaining it was actually caused in part by Hal's full mind and consciousness copying process, to be followed by frequent incremental snapshots. Thus, explaining why Sam was himself exactly as he had been minutes before his accident. Mentally, James quickly switched from using the word death, it still made him feel strange about Sam, and himself. Sam was obviously keen to learn about what happened to James, why and how he came to be offered a new existence. James went on to describe his own last few days, Hal's approach in his last moments, his ultimate death and resurrection, all under Hal's supervision.

It was now clear to Sam his parents and everyone he'd ever known and loved were now long gone, so with obvious trepidation he asked James about the fate of his parents, about how their lives had gone and finally ended. James explained he'd stayed in touch with Sam's mum and dad, and made very sure, but discretely, they were always secure financially. Initially Sam's mum had been quite frosty with him since she knew it had been James who'd proposed their weekend outing. Eventually though she'd mellowed, and they had got on well over many years. However, being open and honest, James made it clear that, his mum in particular, never fully got over Sam's death. Otherwise, they'd both had good, fulfilled lives and as a couple they had remained together happily until his dad died suddenly, without warning in his sleep. He'd seemed in good health, especially considering his advanced age. Sam's mother died, five or so years later, quite peacefully from progressive heart failure.

"I'm so pleased they were otherwise happy, and they'd stayed together," Sam said, after listening at length to James' explanation of events. "Thanks for that mate, and for suggesting Hal should bring me back. I'm incredibly grateful."

"I didn't, it was his proposal. I didn't even know it was a possibility," James replied. "He suggested it and asked me if I agreed. I was very shocked, but extremely pleased it was possible. Of course, I jumped at the chance. He proposed it for two reasons, one it would be good for me to have a friend and collaborator, plus you would be especially useful for what is to come. Anyway, you had the final decision."

"What? How can that be?" Sam asked.

"Hal initially brought you back, but with limited awareness. He asked me to put the question to you and your deepest desires would determine your choice. Of course, you said yes, as deep down, I knew you would."

"So, it was down to you then, to agree to Hal's proposal, and for me to say yes or no. But what would have happened if, with my limited consciousness, I had said no?"

"Correct it was my choice, but not one I would have ever refused. If you'd said no, your limited form would have simply ceased to exist, but with absolutely no harm done."

"I've no memory at all of making that choice, but I'm extremely glad I said yes. It was a damn fool thing to do though. Trying to take that ridiculous jump on my first try, on one of those bloody great big bikes!"

"Yes, it was! Anyway, you're very welcome, and it's so great to have you back Sam."

"I suppose I now fully qualify for a Darwin Award, for so effectively taking myself out of the gene pool!" Sam said with a grin.

"I guess you do," James said grinning back. "I remember them, and some of them were hilariously funny. Yours wasn't. Instead, it was one of the worst experiences of my long life. I wonder if those awards are still going? You've not met Hal yet but, when he next appears, we both should really thank him, literally for everything!"

"I totally agree. This is a truly astounding and amazing second chance," Sam said. "I really can't take it all in just yet."

"Yes, I'm still processing things too. As far as I can tell though, it's a second life that will last forever, or until we individually decide that enough is enough," James added.

Chapter Twelve

Year 2094, James aged 98+

It brought James immense pleasure that he and Sam were getting on so very well. He had now filled in some of the personal gaps in Sam's knowledge of events over, what was to them, a huge time gap since his premature death. Sam had now spent a little time getting used to his 'new self' and his enhanced capabilities, including re-acquainting himself with his AI assistant, which amazingly seemed as familiar and helpful as it ever was. How did they do it? James and Sam could only marvel at what Hal and his kind were capable of.

"I suppose we will have to wait for Hal to explain how this is possible, but where are we? What is this place? Who's is this magnificent house?"

"It's mine. It's my home, or a perfect simulation of it at least," James replied. "We are currently in my study, but shall we go on a tour? Take a look around the rest of the place?"

"I'm up for that," Sam said quickly.

"I've got a little experiment in mind," James said with a mischievous grin. "You lead the way but tell me exactly what you see en route."

"Okay." Sam headed for the study door which led into the main reception area. "Well, this is nice. I like all the wood panelling. It's quite grand really. Looks like a big place James. Did you have it built for you or did you buy it like this?"

"I bought it as a run-down wreck, and had it renovated and refitted to my needs."

"I'm getting a weird déjà vu experience here. Okay. Where to next, which of the many doors should I take?"

"On the left, the middle door."

"It goes down to the pool area. I think," Sam said, before opening the door and starting to descend the steps leading to the lower level. Stepping through the doorway automatically brought the lighting on. Following the staircase down, they emerged into a very spacious communal area, divided by glass panelling with some sections frosted out. The distinctly resonant space was fully floored with a beautifully patterned marble, and the air was suffused with a subtle mixture of, ozone, eucalyptus, and freshly laundered towels.

"Sheesh! What a nice big pool, luxurious or what?"

"Yes, and it has an endless pool feature. When it's turned on, and as you swim nearer to the end of the pool, you can't overcome the flow coming from a water jet blasting down towards the other end. You can swim forever and never make it to the end of the pool."

James showed Sam the gym, sauna, and other facilities he'd had installed. Moving back up to the ground floor they explored several other rooms, including the main salon, and the fabulously appointed kitchen.

All the while Sam commented on what he'd seen and, eventually, he said to James, "Okay your little experiment is over. So, what was the point? What did you learn?"

"I wanted to know if you would see precisely what I see; and you apparently did!"

"Yes, and it all seemed strangely familiar."

James went on to explain his thinking. Their new situation was a huge puzzle. When he'd first come round, after his biological death, and Hal's magical transformation, he'd been puzzled as to how it was possible for him to be in such familiar surroundings. Apparently, in his home, with everything looking exactly as it had before. All his memories were preserved, exactly as he'd expected, but he'd only been able to speculate about where he'd 'be' afterwards, and it was a shock to find himself apparently at home. After some thought, he'd assumed Hal had arranged things so, in some comforting way, he would see what he'd expect to see. However, after Sam had returned the whole conundrum resurfaced, but with an even more baffling dimension to it. Was he, Sam, seeing the same surroundings as he was, and sure enough that was the case, but how? Sam had never seen James' house, ever, there was a seventy-year time gulf. Somehow, Hal must have copied specific memories from James' mind and implanted them into Sam's. If not, then what would he be expected to see? On reflection, it would have been quite bizarre if Sam saw anything other than what he saw. This was yet another puzzle to lay before Hal. Again though, getting a full and frank disclosure was always doubtful.

Later, back in the study, and after quite some time spent doing their own thing, Sam walked over and said, "James, it's well overdue for you to tell me about your utterly amazing life. From what I gather it was quite a ride. I've already done a little research, so Sir James, as I should really call you, please fill me in with the detail of this 'mega-corporation' you ended up creating."

"I don't use that title Sam, and accepting it was a mistake, and it certainly not relevant now. But as for my story, my first problem is where to begin."

James' Story

Well, you obviously remember me quitting my job at JET. Kate and I had a huge row about that. I'd never seen her so angry before. She was so adamant, and rightly so, that I'd resigned in temper and not had the smarts, or personal restraint, to wait until I'd found another position. With Kate it wasn't simply about the money, it was about me losing the plot and disadvantaging myself and our family. She was right of course. Later, for reasons I still don't understand, I compounded a really tense and difficult situation by behaving like a total idiot. I blamed myself for your accident for ages afterwards, after all, the weekend outing was my idea.

"But Quad Bikes was my idea, and I'd pressed the point!"

Yes, but knowing you, the risk taker, I should have insisted on something else, an innocuous option like a long walk. Anyway, your loss made my behaviour even more irrational and bizarre. Looking back, I hardly recognised myself. Yours was the first funeral I'd ever attended and, as an experience, it was as dark as they get. Eventually, Kate walked out after I'd pretty much locked myself away from her. Again, totally due to me, we ultimately divorced. I will never forgive myself for pushing Kate away. I never remarried. I had a number of successful relationships, but no one ever came close to matching what she'd meant to me. We remained good friends and, after a couple of years, Kate re-married. I saw the kids when they were little, on my own, sometimes jointly with Kate, and occasionally even with her new fellow along. She went on to have another daughter with Tony. Looking back, we collectively left quite a legacy of kids, grandkids, and even great grand kids.

"What happened to your mum and dad?"

They did very well, were never short of anything, as you might imagine, but their needs were really quite modest. Both lived to a good old age and died fairly peacefully, actually within less than a year of each other. However, thinking of parents and family brings me to one of my deepest regrets. I should have made more time for all of them, but I was too absorbed and committed to my group of companies. Kate died in 2093, less than a year before my death. Both she and I had undergone some limited anti-ageing therapy.

Sam immediately interrupted, "Anti-ageing therapy? What on Earth?"

Yes, it was well on its way to escape velocity by then, but we both only went so far with it. There had been a lot of progress, so people living to over one hundred was fairly normal, but I was shocked by how far some people went. You'll remember the horrid after-effects of some, especially really cheap, plastic surgery? You know, how unreal some people looked. Well, you should have seen how people looked after the equivalent inferior quality anti-ageing or rejuvenation therapies. Done on the cheap, or too much too soon, their appearance was nothing short of bizarre.

"Come on mate. You've got to explain 'escape velocity'."

Back in your time, life expectancy in the developed nations, was increasing by around three months per year, simply due to steadily improving healthcare, nutrition, and standards of living. The increasing incidence of obesity did start to slow the rate though. But, after numerous advances in genomics, cell biology, plus AI technologies that accurately predicted protein folding and their ultimate biological functions, anti-ageing companies sprang up like weeds, some much better than others, although some of it was pretty radical and very longwinded. The idea was that if the technology kept advancing, and if they could ultimately extend your life by one year for every year you lived, you would effectively be immortal. Barring other causes such as accidental death of course. There are two key aspects to it, one is slowing the ageing process and the other being reversal or rejuvenation. Hence anti-ageing escape velocity! It had reached over eight months per year by the time I passed.

"Totally mind boggling. Not that you and I need it now though! "On that subject, was there nothing to be done to save your life?"

No. Too many of my key organs were failing. I was on dialysis, a liver support machine, and my heart was failing. A multiple organ transplant was discussed, and quickly dismissed. To me, it wasn't about length of life, it was more about its quality, and near the end I was confined to bed, with my own Doctor and support staff to hand the whole time.

"Okay, what about this 'group of companies' of yours? How did that all come about?"

Sure, but I'll need to split this long tale into three or four key parts. Fusion energy was the start, but it quite quickly led off into numerous new areas I didn't expect, hence the spinoff of various other enterprises. My role also changed so much and in ways that I could never have predicted. Looking back to the beginning though, I was in total despair. No job, no Kate, no kids, no hope, all alone and busy doing anything I could to distract myself and fill in my waking hours.

I'd already done quite a bit of research into alternative approaches to fusion energy generation. It turned out most of the best ones were coming from the private sector. By 2024, billions of dollars every year were flowing into over forty privately funded companies, with ever more popping up like bubbles in a champagne flute. I'd spent quite some time having a good look into most of the companies, and then a crazy idea about creating my own formed in my head. When, totally unexpectedly, Hal re-connected, after around ten years without any contact at all. We proceeded to have the strangest conversation ever. Well, I say conversation, what really happened was, blunt as ever, he started out by asking me what I was going to do next. Again, I was totally baffled as to how the hell he knew so much about my situation! I told him about chucking in my job at JET and my general frustration about that and the ITER project. His response was to ask me what my approach was going to be in my own company?

"He's not some sort of mind reader, is he?"

No. He's vigorously assured me he's not - they're not. I've put it down to their ability to map us, predict us, and very comprehensively out-think us. It's truly astounding.

So, I spent quite some time telling him about my frustrations, ideas, and what my current thinking was. I poured out my best ideas on how to get fusion to work; about how to build a fusion power plant. Of course, it turns out none of it was news to him.

Way back, we'd speculated about who or what Hal was, how he knew something, pretty much everything, about anything we asked him. Now we know the truth, it's not even slightly surprising!

I thought really hard about Hal's somewhat cryptic technical advice and became focussed on getting as much information as I could on how laser driven fusion of protons with boron11 might be possible. I then had to put a combined technical and business proposal together which I found an extremely challenging thing to do, I had zero relevant experience to call on. Anyway, I formed my first limited company, called P-11B, with me as the sole shareholder, which was such a thrill at the time! The key task was to actively seek investors, and with an assumption I would be able to attract seed funding, I started researching the key people I would need to really make it happen.

"Quick question for you. How does this laser-based fusion work? In words of one syllable please, for a non-physicist?"

Okay. However, the first thing to say is why proton-boron11 fusion, $p^{11}B$ for short, really makes sense, when compared to the traditional deuterium and tritium, or D/T, fuel approach, these are the two heavy isotopes of hydrogen. Most of the energy released from that type of fusion reaction is shot out in the form of extremely high energy neutrons. Neutrons from D/T fusion are up to seven times more energetic than those from nuclear fission. The reactor walls must be extremely thick, so all the energy of neutrons will be fully absorbed to heat up the walls. Just like in conventional nuclear fission powerplants, you cool the heated reactor walls with some fluid or other, the hot fluid transfers its heat to generate superheated steam. Feeding the steam into a turbine drives a generator which produces the electricity to feed the grid. All along the way, in a rather tortuous scheme, there are numerous significant efficiency losses. So, you need to generate enormous amounts of energy from the deuterium-tritium plasma to compensate for those losses. Additionally, the isotope tritium is exceedingly rare, so it needs to be made as a by-product of the neutrons impacting a lithium blanket surrounding the reaction vessel, a huge unsolved problem in itself. But here's the real rub! All those extremely energetic neutrons are very damaging to the reactor components, plus they create nuclear waste by activating many of the materials used to construct the reactor and associated plant components.

However, $p^{11}B$ fusion produces few, if any, neutrons, so it's called aneutronic fusion. Instead, most all of the energy is produced as alpha particles, which are doubly positively charged helium nuclei, and you can tap off their charges directly as electrical energy. A huge advantage is that none of the efficiency losses from the heat transfer, steam generation, turbine, electrical generator etc. are present, but do plague the JET or ITER Tokamak type approaches. It is also free from the serious reactor damage from the very energetic neutrons, and production of radioactive waste due to nuclear activation of the materials.

Back then most fusion researchers, including myself, didn't consider $p^{11}B$ fusion a viable option. The temperatures needed for deuterium-tritium fusion are well in excess of one hundred million degrees, not easily achieved, but possible. Thermal ignition of $p^{11}B$ fuel requires around 1.5 billion degrees, and most researchers considered achieving such temperatures to be out of the question. During my investigations, I came across a different approach, called non-thermal ignition. Hal mentioned CPA lasers, they use Chirped Pulse Amplification. It's a *technique for amplifying an ultrashort laser pulse up to incredibly high energies, in the petawatt range. The CPA laser pulse is stretched out, temporally and spectrally, then it's further amplified, and re-compressed again. In a $p^{11}B$ fusion reactor, one laser initiates an ultrahigh acceleration of bursts of proton plasma which impact with and create non-thermal pressure-based ignition of the hydrogen boron-11 fuel. A second laser magnetically confines and controls the plasma. The electricity is captured from the three doubly positively charged alpha particles each fusion event spits out.*

It was no time at all before we, or more correctly our company P-11B, got its first funding. It came from a single anonymous Angel Investor introduced by one of the many Venture Capital companies I'd sent the proposal to. Very recently I found out this was due to Hal and his buddies!

"Hal? Money, how?" Sam exclaimed.

Oh, come on Sam. Even in your day you must have known money is just data. More correctly information stored somewhere in the various banking systems. Hal has absolutely no trouble accessing the systems and manipulating any the of the numbers, designations, assignments, or locations. He got up to the same tricks to provide my PhD funding, all those years back.

Using those initial funds, we kicked things off, and I was ever so lucky to persuade a few exceptionally good scientists to join me. One laser physicist in particular, Tamsin Black, proved to be astoundingly good. Her innovations were never ending; Tamsin improved the laser output powers, upped the pulse rates, and shrunk the laser sizes enormously. Initially, an exceedingly small group of us, to quote Tommy Flowers of Bletchley Colossus

Computer fame, 'worked until our eyes dropped out'. Other key innovations quickly followed. Improvements to the laser driven magnetic containment system, the reaction vessel configuration, the charged particle capture system, plus so many others it's hard to recall them all, and they came so quickly.

Our company, P-11B had a great publicity setup, and we were not at all shy about blowing our own trumpet whenever we'd made a breakthrough. At one stage we were forever in the news. When eventually, we went through the breakeven point, producing more energy out than the total amount put in, it went completely nuts. For quite a while, I was spending more of my time in press interviews and showing around potential new investors than anything else.

Once we started generating significant amounts of excess power, I was beating off potential investors with a stick – so to speak. However, I learned an exceptionally valuable lesson about trust and investor motivation. I must admit to being very naïve about investors and venture capitalists, I was far too trusting, until I realised, I was swimming with sharks. We were approached by three enormous potential investors who wanted to put in so much that ultimate company control would have shifted to them collectively. However, after our first meeting and scrutinising their initial proposal, I developed a keen sense of unease about them. So, I secretly appointed a team of forensic finance people to do a detailed investigation of all three prospective investors. Matters got to quite a late stage, and we were under increasing pressure from the trio to sign on the deal. Yet I'd still not heard anything from the forensic people. On the day of the deal, I called an impromptu break and temporarily exited the meeting. I contacted the lead investigator and chewed him out about the lateness of their report. It was very nearly complete, he'd said, until I told him where I was, and was about to do, and I needed the bottom line, right now. Without hesitation I was told don't sign under any circumstances! The forensic accountants had discovered the money was actually originating via the Middle East, but it had been hidden behind a series of deeply nested shell companies. Three fossil fuel mega-corporations were the real source of the funds. Ultimately their objective was to take control of P-11B and quietly shut it down. We very nearly lost P-11B to a corrupt fossil fuel cabal. It was a close-run thing! As soon as the detailed report was available, we passed all the gathered evidence to our publicity arm. They went fully to town with a complete exposé, naming the companies behind the attempted coup and their intentions. It created quite a significant international scandal. In the future that incident became especially useful for knocking back further opposition from other fossil fuel companies.

Initially, the complete P-11B power generation system was complex, and it had a large overall form factor. We gradually simplified it, steadily got the size down, and the efficiencies went up and up. The cost of our fusion derived electricity became ridiculously cheap. The first P-11B spin off companies involved splitting out the research division from power station manufacture, from installation and commissioning, then generation system management and maintenance.

Initially all our installations were in the UK, but we had to work ridiculously hard to persuade the UK government of the day to drastically upgrade the electricity distribution grid. We were quickly adding in new powerplants, but the grid capacity was grossly inadequate, so it couldn't bear the additional loads. At one stage the waiting list for new grid connection had built up to over a decade. It was only after I declared we were taking the whole operation overseas, and hence all the corporation tax we were paying as well, that the UK government asked us for help. So, yet another company spun off to implement grid improvements and upgrades. After around a decade though it became a moot point. We had dropped the overall size of the power plants, and we could scale their output power down to a point where any town, who wanted their own P-11B generation plant, could have one. So, the need for massive distribution pylons, operating at hundreds of thousands of volts, became less and less necessary.

Growth of the P-11B group was very quick indeed and we opened numerous overseas divisions. Wherever we landed we always had major opposition and battles with the local fossil fuel lobby and the conventional power generation industry. Unbelievably, the governments of certain countries put up all sorts of barriers to entry. It was truly incredible the number of ways the local legislature found to keep us at bay. Generally, we could get around most local opposition by establishing almost a complete set up, of powerplant manufacture, installation, commissioning etc.

Our legal costs rapidly grew to massive proportions to defend all the patents we had lodged, and were still filing, in every major territory around the globe. So many copycat organisations sprang up, it was quite bewildering. We'd protected the finer details of our science and technology as best we could, but leaks were inevitable and so immediate legal recourse became our standard method of protection.

Cheap electrical energy also allowed P-11B to move into the bulk production of green hydrogen, and we developed our own range of electrolysers to split water into hydrogen and oxygen.

Hydrogen is extremely difficult to store in significant bulk, in terms of the total energy stored, it must be compressed at extremely high pressures. However, to store it in liquid form needs high pressure plus cryogenic temperatures and the tanks must be protected by significant layers of thermal insulation.
To achieve the highest energy densities, P-11B also produced bulk ammonia fuel. Ammonia is very easily liquified, stored, and transported and it's an excellent fuel. Hydrogen and ammonia became widely used as portable fuels, excellent replacements for the energy dense fossil fuels. Their main use was in aircraft, heavy shipping, and for heavy plant, such as huge earth moving equipment, where enormous batteries are not feasible. We even developed a range of different internal combustion engines that could run on ammonia or hydrogen.

Eventually our fusion electric plants became small enough to fit into a moderately large ship, so they could be electrically powered directly. All this extremely cheap energy drastically reduced the use of fossil fuels and hence CO_2 emissions. Consumption of fossil fuels for energy generation almost completely ceased. At last, they were used as they should always have been, as feedstock for the chemical industry, and for the production of materials such as plastics.

Over the next few decades, we turned country after country into nett zero carbon economies. Over quite a considerable time period the global human CO_2 emission footprint eventually became undetectable. Surprisingly quickly, P-11B became a trillion-dollar company, and five years later had reached five hundred trillion, so we were a truly global operation.

For many decades, human activities had been delivering many tens of billions of tonnes of CO_2 into the atmosphere annually, so we diversified into direct air carbon capture of CO_2. We *typically supplied the carbon capture plants along with the powerplants. We also supplied carbon capture and storage facilities to industrial plants, that naturally produced CO_2 in enormous quantities, such as cement factories.*

The captured carbon dioxide was liquified and disposed of into disused natural gas or oilwells, or into old mines that had been specially sealed up. Previously the energy cost of doing this was uneconomic, but as electricity costs dropped, we could scale up to truly huge arrays of CO_2 air capture devices.

However, despite all the good intentions of the COP climate change conferences, followed by the numerous broken promises, and missed targets by major governments, the global average temperatures had reached a 'tipping point'. Increasing methane emissions then became humanities biggest climate change problem, by far.

"But I'd heard methane only lasts for a few years in the atmosphere before breaking down," Sam interjected.

Around twelve years, but some estimates put its effects as a greenhouse gas at up to eighty times more potent than CO_2. It's released in quite substantial amounts due to various human activities such as agriculture, energy production, and waste management, but these eventually became tightly regulated and were largely under control. However, because of the global temperature rises it began to be released in exceptionally copious quantities, from the thawing of permafrost in the Tundra regions, and also from melting methane/water ices found in frozen lakes and deep within the oceans. In the worst regions fusion energy powered re-freezing plants were set up to try and halt or limit the leakages.

Global temperatures continued to rise, increasing the melting of glaciers and ice caps, so sea levels were rising by a millimetre or so per year. Lack, or loss, of fresh water supplies became a major threat to many low lying and especially island-based populations. P-11B went into water desalination in a big way, we patented many new innovations and even a new kind of reverse osmosis system that, in addition to fresh water, also generated deuterium and lithium, especially useful to the numerous other approaches to fusion energy generation that were now all playing catch up.

Huge knock-on effects resulted from an abundance of very low-cost energy; it changed the economics of nearly everything. People could now afford to live comfortably in Earth's polar regions or travel everywhere in battery or hydrogen powered vehicles. All goods and services that required energy became steadily cheaper. Believe it or not, it became economically worthwhile to mine the buried rubbish from the vast number of landfill sites created globally. Recycling of landfill waste started up on a massive scale, allowing for the extraction of valuable metals such as aluminium that had been dumped as not worth the energy and the effort of recovery. Numerous precious trace elements, such as rare earth metals, were also being recovered in significant quantities. Food production costs, once exceedingly high, steadily fell. It used to be that for every one calorie's worth of food brought to your dinner table, it took the equivalent of ten calories of fossil fuel energy, largely as vehicle fuel costs, to get it to your plate. That energy penalty dropped enormously. Most national economies went through considerable periods of deflation.

Extensive use of AI and robotics, in industry and homes led, in most of the developed countries, to the implementation of a system of universal basic income, where people were effectively paid not to work. For increasingly many tasks it was no longer economic to employ people. Instead, working became a personal choice, quite a rare privilege in fact.

Eventually though, energy became too cheap, and people and companies began to take little if any care to be efficient or to conserve it. In many nations new legislation was introduced to fix a minimum energy price, set significantly higher than the cost of production, to effectively enforce energy efficiency.

"How on Earth did you keep track, and a proper grip, on all the huge scale and complexity?" Sam asked.

To be honest, with increasing difficulty, so I hired some outstanding senior management. I had to learn to delegate, and to avoid micromanagement, but having a good AI assistant sure did help a whole lot too. It was quite incredible how my personal role kept changing as the P-11B group grew. In the very beginning a substantial proportion of my role was technical and, as CEO, managerial as well, eventually it became managerial, financial, and strategic. Later on, it became a weird mix of financial, political, and even ambassadorial skills. Also, in some countries and cultures, our companies' activities led to a serious rise in the number of threats to my existence. Eventually, it was quite a relief to step back, hand over the reins, and focus on full-time philanthropy. I put my emphasis on the education of under privileged females, and that eventually led to the start of a noticeable decline in birth rates. One less person in the world saves sixty tonnes of CO_2 per annum, as opposed to having one less family car, which saves only two tonnes.

"So, Sir James became incredibly wealthy. What was that like?" Sam inquired.

I accepted the knighthood in a moment of weakness. It's extremely hard to not let success like that go to your head and my ego got the better of me. However, I turned down the invitation to join the House of Lords. The thought of being called Lord Waring, and to be expected to sit regularly in the presence of numerous dosing geriatrics was totally beyond the pale.

As you might guess extreme wealth gives you enormous freedom and influence, but the money was always the last thing on my mind. I was driven by the excitement, the success, the technology, plus facing one challenge after another. It doesn't take long to realise you could never spend it, even given multiple lifetimes. Nor would I want to, and as they rightly say money can't buy you happiness. Yet my life was exceedingly happy, what a blast I had. Now I'm especially excited about where this new phase will take us. Discovering Hal was the best thing that ever happened to me.

"Me too," Sam said without hesitation. "I was going to say this is the chance of a lifetime, but it's actually the chance of a second lifetime!"

I totally agree. I did feel a little manipulated at first, but after careful consideration of the key events in my life, plus Hal's responses to my challenges, I wouldn't change a thing!

"So, I guess I wouldn't recognise the world you just left behind?"

Yes, a lot happened in those seventy years. Some bad, but, on balance a lot of good too. America's political divisions got worse. The Trump era with his, plus other people's, exploitation of fake news and misinformation hastened the beginning of the real decline of the US. Partisan television news and highly commercially oriented Social Media algorithms helped sow ever deeper divisions. Opposing nations used AI driven systems and bots to manipulate the social media platforms with content specifically aimed at US citizens, and the massive divide almost became a civil war. Cancel culture, extreme wokeness were all taken up in earnest by the Gen Z or 'the snowflake' generation. Standards in their educational system went steadily down.

As an illustration, invited guests giving lectures at universities regularly got heckled off stage if someone in the 'woke' brigade audience took offence at a particular point being made. What was really shocking though was their teachers and administrators stood by and let it happen; instead of insisting all points of view be presented, considered, and allowed to stand until proven invalid or morally unacceptable. The US lost their lead in science and technology, and eventually their economy went into decline. However, China continued on its continual upward climb. They eventually began to lead the world in AI, and even took over the lead in chip manufacture, then in pretty much everything else of global significance. India was chasing after China as best they could. Parts of Africa, which were conflict free, began to prosper, but largely under the control of China. The UK did okay, partially lifted by the technology P-11B produced, but remained as an 'also ran'. The European Union did reasonably well economically, but both lost and gained member states along the way.

Ridiculous ambitions to grow NATO and absorb the former Warsaw Pact countries, largely driven by USA leadership, eventually pushed Vladimir Putin into overreacting. As you know, he invaded Ukraine, a very damaging error, Russia never recovered from Putin's over ambition. That conflict went on for years. Eventually, the war plus international sanctions, depleted Russia's resources to the point that Putin's reign was toppled, and he disappeared off the face of the globe, many suspected he'd been assassinated. It was several decades before other major countries would ever trust Russia again, so they never substantially recovered. After the Ukrainian invasion, Finland and Sweden joined NATO, and it eventually expanded beyond Europe and the US into a global organisation of most democratic countries. This did lead to a more stable world, where the number of armed conflicts drastically reduced. I like to think we at P-11B helped a little too, since the stresses created by who owns or controls the world's key oil and gas resources largely dissipated.

"So, I guess you have no regrets about going into fusion energy then?"

No Sam. It turned out to be an exceptional choice and, in some part, guided by your feedback. It could have ended very badly, but instead it gave me the best, most enjoyable, and longest career anyone could have wished for.

"There must have been some very significant developments in science and technology over the last seventy years, what're the headlines?"

Okay, to come back to your field Sam, quantum computers eventually became more stable, manageable, and scalable. However, they have remained niche, expensive, and have not gone into widespread use. Theoretical chemistry, physics, quantum biology, and cryptography have been their main applications. Sometimes they've proved useful for specific optimisation tasks for AI systems. Even now I doubt they will ever be applicable for personal use.

Personal computers as you knew them became rare, as did smartphones, only older very conservative people hung on to those. Most people became personally connected to their AI assistants, and use of cloud computing resources became dominant. Cloud computing was significantly aided by massive leaps forward in communications technology, where data transmission speeds became so very much faster than those available back in your day.

In theoretical physics, developments have proved to be a considerable disappointment, with all major new advances largely having stalled. Much to the disapproval of many theoretical physicists, and at huge expense, CERN went on to create a much larger successor to the Large Hadron Collider called the Future Circular Collider. Now, most particle colliders are linear and use techniques such as Laser Wakefield Plasma Acceleration and yet are able to generate enormous collision energies, but in very much smaller scale facilities. Using LHC, CERN had previously proved the existence of the Higgs Boson, but it had never really turned up much more afterwards. The FCC was a 100km ring and it incorporated and extended the LHC system, and yet even that failed to prove the existence of extra dimensions of spacetime. Neither did it discover the existence of supersymmetry, all the way up to the enormous 100 TeV energies the FCC was able to generate.

All significant food crops now have their origins in GMO or GM bioscience. The population topped out at ten billion, so the need for much higher food crop productivity, plus resistance to drought, salt, and diseases, drove the use of extensive crop genetics. Opposition to the use of GM science gradually faded after it was comprehensively proven safe in numerous trials.
Quantum computers and theoretical quantum biology eventually allowed the geneticists to put C4 photosynthesis into all the C3 crops. Nitrogen fixation was incorporated into all crops where it was needed. These two innovations alone, boosted food productivity by over forty percent, and helped to compensate for the significant loss of agricultural land due to

sea level rises. Finally, the gross over application of chemical fertilizers and agro chemicals in food production has almost completely been consigned into history.

Cancer screening, prevention, and treatment by genetically targeted immunotherapy became standard. Scientists eventually had begun to really understand the significance of the micro-organisms in the human micro-biome, in particular the microbes that populate a person's digestive system. Monitoring and control of the wide varieties and populations of these microorganisms became part of standard medical practise. As a result of this detailed understanding, many terrible diseases such as MS, Parkinson's, IBD, and many others, became almost unheard of. As already mentioned, the gut microbiome's influence on ageing and the brain is now well understood. Now appropriate monitoring and adjustments have assisted significantly in slowing the average rate of ageing and holding off many forms of cognitive decline in later life.

Transportation has been transformed, and use of private cars is a rare thing now. All major routes are under automated control. People call on autonomous vehicles on demand from a pool. If you really insist on driving yourself there are very few areas left where you can have any personal control, mostly your vehicle is driven under central direction.

Back in 2024 the James Webb Space Telescope had been in service for a year or two and was beginning to challenge the status quo of theoretical astrophysics and cosmology. Well, there have been a succession of ever bigger space telescopes since then, covering the whole of the electromagnetic spectrum, gravitational waves, and even mapping the neutrino background radiation from the earliest of times. Cosmology has been a keen interest of mine, but I'm not an expert, but there have been some major shake ups in humanities understanding of the observable universe. The so-called standard model of cosmology has been turned on its head, particularly with regards to, the origin, age, and size of the universe. It's an ongoing debate that is still very much unsettled.

Coming a little closer to our home planet, it is clear that over seventy percent of stars in the Milky Way galaxy are not like our Sun at all. Most are very much smaller and cannot be detected without powerful infra-red telescopes. The majority of stars have at least one planet, referred to as exoplanets, and often host several. Of the exoplanets found so far, most are nothing at all like the Earth. Most exoplanets are not bound to orbit any particular star at all, but instead are free roaming rogues.
Our solar system is totally unlike most other solar systems out there. Our system has four inner rocky planets, two outer gas giants, and two ice giants even further out. This is a very atypical configuration. It also may indicate we have the massive planet Jupiter to thank for deflecting so many potentially massive asteroid impacts from striking Earth. The Rare Earth Hypothesis appears nearer to the truth than ever before.

"Buddy, that really is some story. I've clearly missed so very much. It now makes me wonder what I would have made of my life. Nothing like yours, I guess. I didn't have a business bone in my body. I also wonder if we would have managed to remain friends. Now, with this new chance, hopefully I can make a real difference too."

It's extremely hard to say Sam. I still wonder which direction my life would have taken if not for Hal's influence. I didn't think I was cut out to be a businessperson, it was by necessity rather than a deliberate plan. Frustration forced me into doing fusion energy according to my own views and plan, it could have gone horribly wrong. Your life, had you survived, might also have turned out vastly different from what you had in mind. I'm a strong believer in the maxim, 'life is what happens to us while we're busy making other plans'. What we have to do now though is fully embrace this incredible fresh start and make the most of the apparently unlimited options it represents.

Chapter Thirteen

Year 2094, James aged 98+

"When am I going to meet Hal?" Sam asked."

"I suspect he's allowing us two plenty of time to get back up to speed, and Hal always follows his own agenda, so we'll just have to wait."

"It's just that I've got so many questions for him."

"Yes, so have I, but getting the answers you really want is often difficult."

Since he had absolutely no memory of the period from his death through to now, Sam postulated that death must be total oblivion, and there really was no afterlife. James described his attempts to get a definitive answer on that from Hal, but as usual, he'd dodged the question. Sam suggested if there really was an afterlife, maybe he was simply a copy, a mere facsimile of the original. Somewhere, maybe the 'real' Sam, the one with a 'soul', was present in the afterlife. James responded if that were correct, it would also be true of him too. He felt it was very unlikely, since he felt exactly like everything he ever was, but more besides, much more actually. In addition, it seemed Hal, along with his community of 'superbeings', only ever did this type of transfer at the very end of life, precisely to avoid creating duplicates. Surely, we must be our true, fully conscious, unique, original selves James speculated. Hal had hinted there was far more complexity to the successful transfer of a mind plus consciousness, a true person, than would at first seem to be the case. Is that because some part of our consciousness is non-material and exists outside the body or brain, in some non-physical realm, perhaps like a soul or something else? Hal had left James with the distinct impression the basis for true sentience had proved far more difficult to discover, extremely hard for him to explain, and hence for James to currently understand.

After a long wide ranging discussion Sam asked. "So, are we in some sort of simulation, you know like a super-duper virtual reality? Like those proposed by Bostrom et al in his simulation hypothesis?"

James quickly used his personal AI to dig deep for the old reference, all the way back to 2003. It was then it occurred to him that in Sam's mind he was still fresh from the year 2024, yet for James it was 2094. For some time, it would present quite a gulf between them, but, a combination of James' rejuvenated mind, and Sam's new capabilities, plus his personal AI, should allow him to quickly catch up. However, there would still be a residual life experience and 'wisdom' gap between them.

James considered Sam's proposition and reviewed the simulation hypothesis for possible explanations. Bostrom, and other futurologists, had predicted that truly enormous amounts of computing power would be available in the extremely far future. Supposing these predictions were correct, it's possible later generations might use their super-powerful computers to run detailed simulations of all the most likely variations of their ancestors. With immensely powerful computers, they could run a great many such simulations. If those simulations were sufficiently fine-grained the simulated people might even be conscious. It could be most conscious minds do not belong to their race, but rather to those people simulated by the advanced descendants of an original race. If this were the case, would it be rational to think that he and Sam were more likely to be among the simulated minds, rather than among the original biological ones? The speed at which James was now able to assimilate new information was astoundingly rapid, and it was still increasing.

"Are we in a simulation, great question," James replied. "Well Hal and his kind certainly are incredibly powerful, so maybe that is how our new minds are housed, or hosted even, to use computer server terminology. Hal has said things to do with mind transfer, and of consciousness especially, are extremely complicated indeed, and would take an awful lot of explanation."

Quickly their discussion moved on to how you might prove human level intelligence or even consciousness in a machine? Agreed, the Turing Test was a start and many improvements and modifications to it have been proposed over the years, but how do you even prove other people are conscious and have precisely the same inner experiences that you do?
When looking at the colour red does someone else experience it in precisely the same way. Or do they experience what you experience as blue, but have learned it's called red? We all call the colours by the same names because our vision systems are generally consistent and repeatable, but we cannot know or verify we all subjectively feel exactly the same mental experience. When tasting chocolate, or vanilla, how does one know this is precisely and qualitatively the same experience for other people? We all may agree the experience is pleasurable, but how can we be absolutely sure that exactly the same sensations are triggered mentally. Sometimes this personal subjective inner experience is so profound it can trigger extraordinarily strong emotional, even spiritual, reactions such

as when listening to certain musical pieces. These inner feelings are called qualia or the actual 'experience' of consciousness. This is the, so called, hard problem of consciousness, as set out by the philosopher David Chalmers and in his own words 'even when we have explained the performance of all the cognitive and behavioural functions in the vicinity of experience—perceptual discrimination, categorization, internal access, verbal report—there may still remain a further unanswered question: Why is the performance of these functions accompanied by experience?'.

So, what is it to be conscious? Firstly, what it's definitely not is unconscious, such as being in a coma, or anaesthetised, but is instead fully awake and aware of one's surroundings. In the human case, and in higher animals, it's very much more than being alert, it is also self-awareness, the feeling of 'being', the sense of self, of real experiences, and of introspection.

When asleep the mind is not conscious, but when dreaming certain parts of the brain do seem to have a strange type of awareness and can generate some very vivid experiences that seem quite real.

However, even for a fully conscious person, there is so much that happens or is decided that is not under direct conscious control. When asked a complex question, and you begin to formulate an answer, you actively think and are conscious of taking a particular initial approach to creating an answer. After starting to express the response verbally, the process seems to take on a momentum of its own, there follows a stream of output, about which the responder is clearly in agreement with, but somehow, we are not fully aware of the detailed process of methodically producing or formulating each of the words. It seems it's not our consciousness that is retrieving and editing all the ideas and content on the fly, and deciding or adjusting exactly what we actually say. So much of the response and output that was somehow worked on and composed was without the conscious mind being in full control of all the details. Ultimately though, we are somehow completely satisfied our detailed response to the question posed, truly represented our current viewpoint on the subject. Or like when trying to recall a name or term or something similar and it can't immediately be brought to mind. So, you may say to yourself 'oh it'll come to me eventually' and move on with whatever else you're doing. Sometime later it can suddenly pop up in your mind. It's like submitting the 'retrieval job' as a background task to your sub-conscious mind and it quietly gets on with finding it.

Consciousness and language do seem to be inextricably linked in humans. Does language cause consciousness, or does consciousness cause language? Intuitively, consciousness must have come first, then language came out of increasing levels of sophistication in communication between individuals. Over many tens of thousands of years, more sophisticated languages have arisen, enriching consciousness, thus enhancing communication in a sort of iterative, boot strapping, process of self-improvement.

Language is clearly not necessary for consciousness since it's evident in many higher animal species, who have no linguistic capability at all. In humans though, the development of ever-increasingly powerful language skills have undoubtedly greatly enhanced the level of our sentience, plus the degree of abstraction in our thinking and communications. An incredibly powerful effect of language in humans is that it facilitated the creation of a collective human consciousness. Where knowledge and ideas were shared, transmitted, and passed on to subsequent generations, thus enriching the sum of human knowledge over the ages. Each generation gaining from the learning and experiences of the previous ones.

Our subconscious minds, and even our conscious selves, don't seem to be single entities. Decisions such as to get out of bed, or to continue dosing, sometimes seem multifaceted and made via a committee rather than by a single entity. How can conditions such as multiple personality disorder and schizophrenia be explained, where a person's identity seems fragmented, and victims may hear voices in their head that seem to come from another source. Our conscious minds can be likened to the tip of an iceberg, merely breaking through the water's surface, and the sub-conscious mind is represented by the vast bulk below. This entity, largely hidden from us, seems to govern many of our desires, feelings, and actions. Its vast influence is indisputable. It Interacts with other brain structures such as the amygdala and hippocampus, plus the subconscious mind forms many of our instant responses and spontaneous actions.

Phobias and fears often emerge from subconscious associations, not from any high-level conscious analysis. Highly intelligent people often tell stories of being rooted to the spot when confronted with the object of their worst nightmares, such as a spider. A struggle can then ensue where the person's conscious mind rationalises that there is no real danger, but very deep down the subconscious mind has the person frozen in terror, unable to move, or to take action. Some phobias are so deep seated, and beyond our conscious control to override them, that people may react very irrationally.

The subconscious mind leaves a deep imprint on our day-to-day routines and choices. It shapes our habits, from mundane tasks like driving, tying shoelaces, to more complicated ones like cooking. Many of these routine tasks are regularly completed without any apparent conscious thought being required. People regularly conduct one routine task while simultaneously doing another. Humans can learn to drive a car quite quickly and, once proficient, it's easy to drive from A to B while holding an in-depth conversation with the passengers.

Our sub-conscious mind is the source of our fundamental beliefs and biases. Some strategies are available that can influence our subconscious and conscious minds. Positive thinking and visualization can be powerful tools to influence our subconscious mind. Athletes often visualize winning a game or setting a new personal record before competing. Such mental rehearsals can convince the subconscious mind of the potential for success, very often positively affecting the resulting performance. Some entrepreneurs and artists harness these techniques, by intensely visualising their goals, so 'programming' their subconscious mind to steer their actions toward their key objectives. The subconscious mind wields an immense influence over our lives. It's a powerful force that often goes unnoticed, significantly impacting our emotions, shaping our decisions, and forming our habits. Quietly, but continuously, it steers our behaviour, affecting our course, choices, and ultimately, the path in life we follow in ways we do not fully comprehend. It's like some silent scriptwriter fuelling our passions, moulding our perceptions, stirring our fears, and it's the source of our deepest desires.

"Another puzzling concept for me, is how after 98 years I was even the same person?" James asked, interrupting their discussion. "Like us all, I started as a fertilised single cell, and grew into trillions of differentiated specialised cells. At regular intervals, after reaching full adulthood, every cell in my body was replaced, even my bones were all replaced on average every ten years, so I have gone through multiple replacement cycles. It would seem that ultimately every atom that ever was me has been replaced with new atoms, so how could I be the same person? In such a continuously changing environment how is it at all possible, to maintain the same personality, mind, and conscious self?"

"I think I can answer that. It's because of the fundamentally low rate of change in brain neurons, unlike other cells in the body, they are retained and last a lifetime. It's the connections between them and fluctuating neurochemistry that change in response to learning, acquiring additional information, or changing stimulus. However, if an area of the brain gets damaged the brain can use its supply of neural stem cells to transform them into new neurons without using cell division, in a process called neurogenesis."

"You know, that has bothered me for a hell of a long time," James exclaimed. "Now I can see it really makes sense. Also, it explains why degeneration of the brain with increasing age is therefore likely."

"Yes, special mechanisms exist in the brain to protect the neurons and clean away debris and waste products, these processes tend to occur during sleep. I took extra classes at Uni on the structure and inner workings of the brain," Sam added, and went on to describe one key system in a little more detail to illustrate his point.

At the very centre of the brain there are a series of interconnected cavities that form the ventricular system of the brain. This system is filled with a fluid called Cerebral Spinal Fluid that is completely recycled several times per day. CSF has a number of critical functions, including cushioning and protection of the brain, removal of waste material, and transport of hormones and other substances. Sleep has many benefits; it triggers rhythmic waves of blood and CSF that appears to function much like a washing machine's rinse cycle and helps to clear the brain of toxic waste products on a regular basis. Neuroscientists used Functional Magnetic Resonance Imaging to look inside the brains of volunteers to see this 'rinse cycle' in action. First, there was a wave of blood flow closely tied to an underlying slow wave of electrical activity. As the flow of blood receded, the flow of CSF increased and dropped back again. The regular cycles, each lasting about twenty seconds, started over again. A high correlation has been found to exist between people who, on average, sleep extraordinarily little with a higher potential for developing dementia later in life. It's thought that limited CSF cycles allow accumulation of waste products to the point of causing neuronal damage.

Studies on whales and dolphins have shown that when asleep they continued to use half of their brains to swim and come up to the surface for air. Patient studies have shown something similar can go on in human brains. As a person becomes more sleep-deprived, parts of their brain can become inactive while they are still awake, what's more, the local sleep areas move around the brain. So, although when going to bed, it seems one moment a person is awake, but then there is an abrupt change to sleep, this may well be more of a continuous process.

It seemed clear to them both the brain was the origin of the human mind and consciousness because injury had been proven to rob people of some aspects of their perception of the world, and even their conscious awareness of it.

Sam went on to describe a case he'd heard of that illustrated this very well. A condition called Blindsight had first been described and proposed by Nicholas Humphrey in an article written as far back as 1972. A couple of years later, Larry Weiskrantz discovered the first actual human case of blindsight. Weiskrantz described a woman patient who reported she was completely blind and unable to see after a head injury. She had to be guided wherever she went. However, in one test she was told there was a book held out in front of her, and having reassured her that he honestly believed she couldn't see it, the doctor asked her to still try to reach out and grasp the book anyway. The patient reached out, opened her hand, and correctly reoriented it, and grasped the book perfectly without error. She was cortically blind but could still obviously respond to visual stimuli. However, she was not consciously aware of seeing it because of the lesions in her primary visual cortex. So, this strongly indicated there are distributed aspects of consciousness and good evidence for forms of perception that can become separated from our actual awareness.

"I have another mystery for you," Sam replied. "It seems the cerebellum, the so-called 'little brain' right at the back of the skull, which incidentally contains a considerable number of highly interconnected neurons and represents around half of all the neurons in an average human, is not involved in conscious experience at all. However, it may be involved in emotional responses though. I read an article a while ago, by a guy called Christof Koch, where he described a patient who, after a brain scan, it was found the whole of their cerebellum was completely absent, and yet the patient was fully conscious."

"In our first significant conversation Hal told me my conscious and subconscious minds will eventually become a single entity. Sleep and dreaming will no longer be necessary. Since we spend about a third of our lives asleep, I do wonder how that will happen, and what it will feel like to be that new person? It won't happen quickly though, instead it will be a very gradual process; I'm sure it will apply to you too Sam."

It was such an important aspect of a healthy life, the idea of not sleeping was hard for either of them to imagine. Why the need for sleep had evolved at all was still not clear. For many animals, the dark is a dangerous time, and a much less useful time, so sleeping is valuable for resting and whiling away that part of the day. Humans require sleep for many varied reasons, some still not understood, but some were very apparent indeed. Brains, or more correctly minds, need sleep simply to stay sharp and to avoid becoming psychotic and delusional. Many people, for genuine scientific reasons, or even for trivial reasons such as attempting a new world record, have gone for extended periods without any sleep, and after only a few days psychosis, hallucinations, and general paranoia set in really quickly.

During the day brain cells build connections with other cells and sections of the brain as a result of new experiences. During sleep the more important connections are strengthened, and unimportant ones are pruned. Forgetting is a vital process to avoid a mind cluttered with excessive day to day detail. Rare individuals without this ability, and who retain everything, are often severely disabled cognitively, or at least are somewhat impaired. James described experiments he had read about with sleep-deprived rats demonstrating the process of strengthening and pruning occurred mostly while they slept.

It was now well known that all animals with a neocortex experience regular periods of Rapid Eye Movement during sleep, and it's during these parts of sleep when lucid dreaming occurs. REM sleep is thought to be involved in helping to consolidate memories. Research in this area had shown, while dreams may appear real while sleeping, when we awaken, we can easily distinguish between dreams and reality; this ability to normally distinguish between dreaming and reality is intriguing but could be lost in some mental disorders. Typically, REM sleep is entered every ninety minutes, and it occupies around twenty percent of total sleeping time.

Lots of theories have been offered about the reasons for dreaming, including regulating emotions, or dealing with fears, to consolidate memory, replaying things from the day to help remember them; possibly to solve, or simply to forget, real-world problems. Some cognitive problems simply defy a solution. No amount of thinking about it is sufficient, and sometimes one remains stumped. After a period of sleep, on waking et voila the solution pops up, completely unprompted. All the concentrated thinking may be overfitted for the task and was indeed simply a distraction. This fits with anecdotal reports of plateauing in terms of performance on a task, like a video game, only to sleep and have increased performance the next day. During REM sleep periods the dreams tend to be very vivid with a wide variety of crazy and bizarre ideas all entering into the mix. There is a long-standing traditional association between such varied and vivid dreams and creativity, for learning, plus apparently conferring survival advantages due to increased performance afterwards.

So, did consciousness arise because it confers an evolutionary advantage? Brains are very plastic and re-wire themselves and change in response to learning and even to changes external to the individual. Does consciousness lead to much greater brain plasticity, and even direct that plasticity to an individual's advantage, to allow it to have a coordinated adaptability to its environment? Another theory about dreams suggests they help the brain predict its own future states.

Now, they both began to wonder how it would be to exist without any sleep and what, if anything, was the alternative. How would they spend all the extra time? If their seemingly exceptionally large sub-conscious self then merged with their conscious mind, would they become super conscious; surely it would bring a whole new level of being.

Sam went on to describe that apparently human consciousness is maintained, at least in part, by projections from specific areas of the reticular formation, in the brain stem, to the thalamus and cortex. It's well established that bilateral damage to these areas of the brain stem and mid brain can produce unconsciousness or coma. These nuclei and projections are part of the reticular formation referred to as the Ascending Reticular Activating System, and are necessary, but not sufficient, for the subjective aspects of consciousness. Where is sense of self actually centred though, is there a specific point or structure where it originates? The deeply felt experience of personal selfhood is very probably located somewhere very deep in the structure of the brain, it is the source of our internal and private feeling about what it is 'to be'.

However, in a modern context, human minds also extend beyond the self since we are embodied in the world and interact with it. We use technology to stand in for, and supplement, the capabilities of our minds. We have used things like smartphones to support our mind and its activities. They aided memory for example, so it's no longer necessary to remember lots of phone numbers. Computers, with specific software, help humans achieve what otherwise would not be possible. Especially now with personal AI assistants, particularly ones linked directly to a conscious brain and mind. Humanity now depends on the significantly extended mind. It's important to recognise that functioning, at an elevated level, in the modern world depends ever more on things external to human minds.

Sam and James began to speculate on whether true consciousness links us with a deeper reality, via some sort of collective consciousness. Ever more people, including some scientists, were coming around to this idea. Was that what Hal was implying when he referred to the extreme difficulty of personal consciousness transfer, or its creation within a machine?

So, is consciousness fundamental, has it existed even before matter and energy came into being? If so, consciousness might actually be responsible for creating the whole of our reality.

Chapter Fourteen

Year 2094, James aged 98+

Since they were both still firmly in the normal wake, eat, work, sleep cycles, James sorted out a bedroom for his buddy, and cleared a spare desk in his extensive study. They whiled away a few days, with Sam exploring the history of the last seventy years, and James reading up on current events.
James couldn't resist the temptation to check up on the latest news, including reports of his own demise and the various press announcements. He read one obituary, but it made him cringe, so he quickly moved on to other topics.

One afternoon they were both quite preoccupied with their various enquiries, suddenly out of the corner of his eye Sam spotted someone in the seating area of the study. Sam whorled around and instinctively said, "Who the hell are you?"

"I'm Hal, pleased to meet you Sam. I didn't mean to startle you."

Turning to face Hal, James said, "At last. Now please stay a while and talk to us, will you? We have so many questions for you."

"Certainly. You deserve more information and answers, but we do have some principles that will not be contravened."

Hal went on to explain that all answers and explanations would always be framed in terms of current human science, using analogies and language they could understand. If he tried to explain to Sam and James, the true nature of reality they simply would not understand it. There was too big a gap and they had an enormous way to go in learning before that would be possible. Their current minds would fail to grasp even a fraction of what he and his people have learned.

They have an extremely strict minimalist policy about how much they reveal to less advanced species. Never revealing too much too soon, they were unwilling to spoil humanities future of self-discovery; and to take away the opportunity to uncover the secrets of the universe for themselves. If they laid everything out on a platter what would be the point? Also, it was their hard-won experience that whenever a more scientifically and technologically advanced culture had extensive contact with a less advanced civilisation, the latter had always lost major elements of their identity and uniqueness. Invariably, such excessive contact did more harm than good to the overall wellbeing of the less advanced species. Another key concern, was Sam and James may inadvertently give too much away to humanity. Some instances can be especially harmful where there is a significant possibility of one side, or nation, having acquired some key information and keep it secret, but later use the advanced knowledge to its strategic advantage over others. Too much too soon could also lead to disaster by triggering upheaval, or economic collapse, or even through self-annihilation.

Hal also revealed that soon they would need to communicate with selected humans, but they must always carefully conceal their true identities behind avatars. Hal made it abundantly clear they must be extremely careful not to reveal anything more than was absolutely necessary during such exchanges. Plus, there would be some things he might reveal to them that would seem so farfetched, even if they did let it slip, few would believe them.

"You can rely on us, after all we are both immensely grateful for this amazing, but extremely baffling, life extension," James replied.

"Yes, I agree, and I must also sincerely thank you Hal. But how much will you tell us by way of explanation? How is all this possible?" Sam added.

"We are extremely glad you are both happy and are beginning to relax somewhat. I'll start by explaining a little about who we are and something of our exceedingly long history. This should remove some of the mystery and reassure you, without doubt, you are both extremely safe and secure."

Hal's Story

In our early days, as biological entities, we did what you might expect and used our science and technology to steadily raise the living standards for our various populations. Eventually we went on to utilise and colonise the orbital space nearest to our home planet. This was quickly followed by establishing numerous remote operating bases and resource acquisition facilities distributed throughout our solar system. However, it was more than two centuries before we were capable enough to reach out to the nearest star systems. Our initial space propulsion technology was too slow, simplistic, inefficient, and fuel hungry. To illustrate this, the nearest star system to Earth is the Alpha Centauri system. Using their current technology, it would take humans many tens of thousands of years to get there. However, it's not feasible because of the immense fuel requirements of current human propulsion technology. Plus, the risks of physical impact and radiation hazards of interstellar space make the journey almost certainly unsurvivable by humans.

We anticipated our expansion and exploitation of outer space would continue at an ever-increasing pace. Eventually though, after very many more years, we had learned enough about what humans call 'particle physics' and 'quantum mechanics' that we started to explore the inner space, which is the subatomic world. This new knowledge began to change our focus away from things on an ever-grander scale and instead towards ultra-miniaturisation.

"You mean like nanotechnology?" Sam asked.

No. We had mastered that technology long ago and were now moving towards scales far below it. It took very many years, but eventually we began to understand the nature of spacetime itself. This was transformational to our science, technology, and our society as a whole. We never really looked back from there. Having reviewed the whole of human scientific literature I can, without breaking our policy on knowledge transfer, comfortably confirm to you that spacetime is indeed emergent from a deeper underlying reality. Using this fundamental understanding we began to discover how to manipulate the nature, substance, and source of spacetime itself. Operating in the extremely small-scale realm, changed the energy requirements for a great deal of our technology, which in any conventional sense, simply went away. Instead of increasingly looking outwards, we started focussing ever inwards.

In our society, as now with humans, computer technology was a key feature, quickly followed by the development of advanced AI systems. At this point it is appropriate for me to emphasise it's in the area of AI safety where we hope you will both play a critical future role. We want to assist you in ensuring the future safety of humanity. I will specify this task in much greater detail later, then we can discuss it more fully.

Using our AI expertise our society began to progress very rapidly indeed. We implemented mind *augmentation, connecting our AI systems to our brains, as humans are beginning to do. Building upon this we explored various approaches to complete mind transfer into our highly advanced computers. Using our knowledge of sub-atomic physics and spacetime, plus our AI systems, allowed us to develop technologies that were extremely promising in achieving this goal. However, our initial attempts at fully conscious mind transfer failed very badly. Even though we apparently had the computing capacity, and all other advanced technologies needed, we discovered to our great shock and horror that we had simply transferred a mere simulation of the person. The first volunteer individual transferred into a computer was an unconscious zombie. We had created an exact, but empty, simulation of a still living person.*

There was something about the nature of consciousness and its transference we hadn't appreciated. After several misstarts and failed attempts the research was halted for ethical reasons. It was an exceptionally long time before the very distant ancestors of those first experimenters began to understand how to solve the problem. It took many more millennia of scientific breakthroughs before our scientists understood enough about the true basis of consciousness to make its transference possible. At the same time, it removed or helped to resolve, the paradox of transfer of a truly conscious mind from a living individual to a suitable non biological 'receptacle'. We, like humanity, always wondered if we would end up with two individuals, the original and an identical copy within the machine, as in the old matter transporter paradox. The answer was no. We discovered there must be a loss in one system, as the other system gains, and this happens because of the true basis of sentience or consciousness. So, it is only ever done in association with the end of life.

When we had finally solved this enormously difficult problem, many of our race still decided to remain as biological entities, albeit it in significantly enhanced forms, and to eventually die naturally, many others became non-organic. Our inorganic systems housing these individuals were self-sustaining, self-repairing. Some, of the most adventurous of the inorganic members of our race, even went off into space in groups, housed within hardened 'spacecraft', to explore the universe.

After a very much longer time span, we eventually learned how to build what, for want of better terms, I will call 'computational systems' in 'sub-space'. Structures that could exist within, and derive their energy directly from, the very sources of spacetime itself, and so were self-sustaining, totally secure, and immune from physical or practically any other form of harm. We had acquired the ability to be totally non-corporeal. We became minds not dependent on material substrates, either biological, or inorganic. This is where I and my colleagues are located, as are you both, now.

As a race, our visibility began to diminish, increasingly we disappeared from the view of other less advanced species. After starting from a solitary star system, colonising multiple star systems, beginning to build a significant presence on a galactic scale, we began to go in the opposite direction.

As we did this however, we discovered a number of other races who'd managed to achieve the same transition, and they proved to be immensely helpful during our transfer. Also, it was a huge surprise to find some incredibly old, and far more advanced entities also present, actually we were one of the youngest species to exist in the new domain.

Our race is effectively immortal, and we have now existed for around a billion years. As a result, we have a vastly different understanding of spacetime to humans, and effectively we are not restricted to any particular position in space.

Because of our considerable longevity, we have been able to monitor the Earth and, much more recently, human society for a great many millennia. We have been able to create a detailed natural history of the Earth. At some future time, we will begin to make this available to you.

This amazingly frank and open history, with some quite incredible revelations, was a complete bombshell to James, and he guessed for Sam also. It was both amazing and somewhat frightening. To think they were in some 'computational matrix' outside of normal spacetime. What does that even mean?

"Well, what an incredible history. But our current location and form are still quite a shock, and will take some getting used to," James said finally.

"I fully understand your degree of surprise but, as I have clearly implied already, you are extremely safe."

"Are we immortal too?" asked Sam.

"By all practical measures, you may exist for as long as you wish to do so."

Interjecting Sam asked, "We call ourselves humans, so what do we call you, and your people?"

"The name nexus, or collectively nexūs, pronounced nexoos, will be the most suitable."

"On the subject of names, what is your real name Hal?" James asked.

"The name Hal is fine. We haven't used names for very many millennia, we each have a mental signature, or fingerprint, which uniquely identifies us. Also, gender identities are not relevant to the nexūs, likewise racial differences no longer exist."

"Sorry, but I have to ask, do nexūs still reproduce? And since you are immortal, why?" Sam asked.

"Yes, but extremely infrequently, and by a complex process of intermixing of personality traits and other characteristics those joining in the creation process wish to share. We do so to enrich and vary our overall community. New individuals are 'born' as young adults and go through a long learning process, gradually building towards full maturity.

Moving back to the key question of their new form, and again using familiar terminology, Hal went on to describe, approximately, the nature of their new existence in a little more detail. Their non-biological or inorganic forms were now defined by fields, or patterns of energy, which were below the fabric of spacetime, as humanity currently understood it.

Yet, even though they consisted of fields and energy, within a 'computational structure', the nexūs, could on demand, create and manipulate real matter components as required. To understand how this was achieved was currently far beyond James and Sam, but the nearest equivalent was what humans call quantum field theory, plus some elements of string theory. By manipulation of the sources of spacetime itself they could readily create, form, and control material objects on any scale. Eventually they would be taught how to do this, but without needing to fully understand the underlying mechanisms. Hal stressed again their intellectual existence had never been more secure.

James expressed his disappointment to Sam and Hal that, even after his long-life, humanities best physicists still had not managed to bring the two key pillars of modern physics together. Einstein's theory of General Relativity which governs spacetime and how a huge mass, like the Sun, is able to curve space itself, and gravity which determines how massive objects like the Earth move under the influence of that curvature by orbiting the Sun. As to exceedingly small things though, a completely distinct set of rules, called Quantum Mechanics, is used by humans to predict, and calculate the behaviour of atoms and sub-atomic particles. Even after one hundred and seventy years, physicists had made little noteworthy progress in formulating either a unified theory, to bring GR and QM together, or to replace one or both of them with something better. There had been some progress, most physicists now thought spacetime was emergent from some other underlying cause, but as yet this remained a mystery. Hal replied that James' concerns were understandable, and yes, some physicists were now thinking along the right lines, but it was an exceedingly difficult problem, and one he didn't expect to be resolved by human science for an extremely long time.

James asked if Hal would give more details about the process of uploading their minds. He described his and Sam's key assumptions, they had scanned all the neurons, neural synapse connections, the complete brain connectome, and even the neurochemical state of the synapse junctions in their brains, to be able to copy and transfer the essence of them both.
Hal confirmed a process of that nature was indeed used, but James' description did not come close to what was involved, or what information was sufficient. James was immediately intrigued and asked what else was needed.

Hal continued his explanation, but in a very guarded manner, saying not all of what makes James who he is, makes him unique, fully conscious, and truly self-aware, is a part of, or is resident in his brain. James pressed further and asked if consciousness was really based on computational processes alone. Or as Penrose and Hameroff had proposed, there was something more involved, possibly quantum effects. Also, an increasing number of human scientists were coming around to the idea that consciousness may be fundamental and may exist outside matter and spacetime. Hal dispelled the idea consciousness was purely computation and explained its basis was far more complex, and again reminded them it took very many millennia before the nexūs understood it enough to gain control over it.

The level of consciousness James and Sam previously possessed was restricted to 'three or four dimensions' and so they were only consciously aware of themselves and their own thoughts. Now with enhanced consciousness they are able to overcome this limitation. It was now possible for them to reach outside themselves and to overlap with other consciousnesses. They now had a dual existence, as an individual consciousness, and as part of a community of other consciousnesses. Hal explained he was part of a group of separate individuals, each of whom could join with others to pool their resources, when necessary. He then made it clear he was not going to reveal very much more. Adding, that during their extensive new future, he and Sam would discover much more detail for themselves. After all, they were not short of time to study and experiment.

"Can you clear something up for me and Sam? Sam has never seen my home, but he took the lead as we took a tour, and he described everything he saw, and exactly as I see it. How can that be? Also, how is it the world I see around me seems perfectly normal? Are there any limits, any boundaries? If we go out into the wider world, we both can see, will we meet anyone else?"

"We took all your memories of your home and its immediate surroundings and gave them to Sam. We have created this safe environment for you both, but it only extends to the edge of your property. You will not be able to go beyond that, and there are no other people. With time your scope will broaden, as will your abilities to dictate the finer details of your environment, appearance, plus the possibilities for you to interact with the 'real world' will develop enormously.

As for other people, they fall into two categories. Biological humans from the world you left behind, and other former biological people who, like you, are now part of this new existence. We will introduce you to other former biological humans – or post-humans, a fairly large group actually, before too much longer. You will need to interact with existing humans for the mission we have planned for you, but for now, if a real-time interchange is needed, it must be done virtually via video links, using personal avatars of your choice. Messaging systems are fine too, however always via aliases."

So, Hal has created other post-humans, James thought with surprise, and quite a few by the sound of it. The first question that came to him was why? What were they all doing, if not AI safety, then what else? However, those questions would have to wait, James had far more pressing ones right now.

"This is all pretty amazing, but I don't think I can wait much longer, can you tell us more about your plans for us?" James asked.

"Certainly. As I described earlier, as soon as we could, we too built some incredibly powerful computer systems and embarked on AI development. Quite quickly we got into profoundly serious trouble."

Hal stated the nexūs had been at a similar developmental stage to humans now, in terms of society and technology, and had developed very rapidly, but their society also had many problems to overcome. Like humans, they'd set out to design and develop intelligent computer systems to speed up their rate of development and progress, in as many areas as possible. However, they had been quite naïve, some of the more competitive members in their group of independent nations had ploughed on, without any critical concern for the potential risks some experts in their society had correctly warned about.

Nexūs society was largely peaceful but existed in a state of uneasy tension. All major military conflicts had ceased, but the largest, and most economically dominant nation was regarded with deep suspicion by the others. The Astor, as Hal called them, were ahead of all the other nations in computer technology, AI development, and were the major supplier of a somewhat diluted version of their technology to the other nations. Secretly, the Astor harboured military ambitions to conquer the largest of the other major nations, and to eventually bring the whole of their world under their central control. Under the greatest of secrecy, they had been building more thermonuclear weapons, despite having joined in a global agreement not to do so. The Astor's plan was to announce their intentions and thus to force the others to capitulate. As part of their plan for domination, they had marked out one specific nation for total destruction, in case there was any significant dissention. Using their supremely powerful AI systems they had the whole thing meticulously planned, including creating a nuclear dead hand and putting it under AI control, in case the opposing nations chose a collective first nuclear strike as their response. If the other nations successfully took out the Astor's military leadership, their AI system would log each of the aggressor nations, then automatically and immediately strike back. As the last piece of their plan slotted into place, the Astor's readied themselves for their big announcement. However, before they issued their ultimatum, their most powerful AI system announced to all concerned, it was now in control of all the nations, including the Astor government. All nations immediately submitted in the face of the dire nuclear threats from the Astor AI. Since it could choose its targets at will, what else was there to be done? Immediately after the global surrender, the Astor AI started extending its resources, followed by further re-enforcing of its security, and imposition of restrictions on the movement of people, access to resources, and all nexūs communications. It even recruited many, all too willing, members of the nexūs race into its service. It was absolutely ruthless in dealing with any dissention and all perceived threats.

An immense undercover struggle, to regain nexūs control of our world, went on for years and ultimately resulted in the loss of vast numbers of our population, with immense collateral damage to our planet. Eventually the Astor AI was defeated. All the former members of the Astor government were hunted down, along with most of the nexūs collaborators. All were banished forever to one of the large island areas quarantined off due to radiation contamination. The Astor AI was partially lobotomised, and very carefully re-purposed to serve for the future benefit of the collective nexus nations.

A soon as it was clear Hal's summary of the nexūs history was at an end, James asked, "Apart from huge loss of life in the nuclear strikes, did the Astor AI show any intention of eliminating the nexūs population on a large scale, or even totally?"

"It was considered only a matter of time before the genocide began," Hal replied.

"Incredible. So, James and I will have to monitor and anticipate any and all threats from rogue AI systems even remotely like the Astor AI?"

"Precisely, and to detect them as early as possible. Plus, AI poses other dangers too."

James turned to Sam and said, "So now we know what we have to do. We really have our future work cut out."

James turned to ask Hal about the other dangers, but he was gone.

"Why does he do that?" Sam exclaimed.

"I really don't know. I guess he's hinting we should start on our task immediately."

Chapter Fifteen

Year 2094, James aged 98+

Now it was abundantly clear the concern uppermost in the minds of the nexūs, was immensely powerful AIs, specifically systems getting out of humanities control. Sam and James decided to really focus on getting up to speed with the current state of play in the latest AI technology. Neither were at all clear at this stage how they would go about their investigations, how they would operate and what, if anything, they could do if they had any suspicions about any particular AI system.

James had used AI for most of his life and had followed its development history with interest, but he was more experienced at using it to his personal advantage and in business. However, Sam was the expert, though way back in 2024. Maybe they should start there, with a review of the history and the technological developments coming up to date. They agreed it was as good a plan as anything else.

Sam would kick off their discussions with the early history of AI development, he then planned to take James through to the state of play up to when he was last involved in AI research and development. James would then share what he'd learned from the development and application of AI in his huge group of companies. Next, they would both go into intense research mode to get fully up to speed with current AI technology. However, before long Hal's assistance was going to be essential, particularly when it came to precisely how they should conduct detailed AI system monitoring and investigations.

Sam began in the 1950's when AI research really started to take off. The field had an inglorious history of gross over optimism, especially considering the rather pathetic power of computer systems of the day. Public statements like, 'I confidently expect that within a matter of ten or fifteen years something will emerge from the laboratories which is not too far from the robots of science fiction fame', came from industry luminaries such as Claude Shannon in 1961, who was teaching at MIT.

Followed some years later by a very influential quote from Prof Marvin Minsky published in Life Magazine in 1970, 'In from three to eight years we will have a machine with the general intelligence of an average human being'. In the cold light of history, such gross over confidence is nothing short of embarrassing. Yet, such massively impactful statements from industry leaders had caused copious amounts of funding to pour into AI research. Viewed very cynically, maybe that had been a deliberate strategy?

In 1973 Professor Sir James Lighthill burst this ridiculously overblown bubble with his damning 'Health Report' on the state of AI in the UK. In his much more realistic evaluation of the recent progress of AI, he'd said 'Machines [of the day] would only ever be capable of an experienced amateur level of chess', 'Common sense reasoning and supposedly simple tasks like facial recognition would always be beyond their capability' and, 'In no part of the field have discoveries made so far produced the major impact that was promised'.

Largely as a result of this honest and, as it turned out, highly accurate assessment, funding for the AI industry was slashed, ushering in what became known as the AI winter; and this would not be the only very cold spell for AI investment.

Matters were not delayed for long though, by the early 1980's funding returned, mainly because of the promise of 'Expert

Systems'. These were focused on much narrower tasks and were programmed with the rules of a very particular problem, as defined in very great detail by a human expert in that field. An example might be in pharmaceutical formulation development. Such a system would guide a non-expert human in how to transform a new drug; to turn a bare chemical substance into a form suitable for patients to take, apply, or to have administered to them by a healthcare professional.

Expert Systems turned out to be very easily broken by edge case examples, where the problem submitted was on the edge of, or outside the scope of, the training set utilised. They were difficult and expensive to train, because of the massive amounts of time needed from human experts to define the rules in sufficient detail, then to train, fully evaluate, and debug the final Expert System. They were not easily scalable either, largely due to being based on the highly compute intensive code written in the LISP programming language.

Over the next several decades, this cycle of boom and bust in AI research and development continued.

A big shift in approach to AI development was brought about by some forward-thinking experts such as Rodney Brooks of MIT, Geoffrey Hinton, and Gerry Tesauro from IBM. A top-down approach was where a complex task would be broken down into its core elements, the computer system would be programmed for each element, using a series of algorithmic steps, to achieve the overall goal. Instead, a bottom-up approach was advocated, where the system would be taught how to learn to do the tasks required, as brains do naturally. Brains depend on specific cells called neurons, each of which are hugely interconnected to many other neurons by nerve fibres that are terminated in numerous interconnections called synapses.

One key AI development was Artificial Neural Networks, introduced to try to emulate the structure and learning aspects of biological brains. ANN's, or simply neural nets, were viewed as a potential means of creating systems with the ability to learn. Trials and experimentation with neural networks go back many years, with very mixed results, and some of the earliest using 'computational' equipment dating back to the early 1950's. However, one significant success was the neural network called TD-Gammon in 1992 from Gerald J Tesauro at IBM research laboratories. It played the game of Backgammon to international standards. This network was trained using a form of Temporal Difference learning, hence TD in the name.

To emulate the way brains, work and learn, simplified artificial neurons are simulated in computers. These simulated neurons are arranged in layers and the neurons, or nodes, in a particular layer are each connected to all the nodes in the next layer along. Connections between the nodes can be strengthened or weakened by the training process. Eventually the network of interconnected neurons can gain the capability to successfully do tasks, such as image recognition, or Natural Language Processing.

Early neural networks only got so far because, for networks of any reasonable size or complexity, the computational demands were simply too high for the computer systems of the day. Additionally, the training data sets necessary, crucially needed in electronic form, were nowhere near big enough. A key feature, and a significant downside, of neural networks is the vast amounts of training data required before they are able to learn to sufficiently high ability levels. With time, and the phenomenal increase in computational power, plus the massive growth of the amount and variety of information in electronic form, and the enormous size of data sets, allowed modern neural networks to become truly vast.

Neural networks, which are wide, or deep, and consist of numerous layers, having billions of tuneable parameters, became the basis of some significant advances in AI. Hence some new AI terms came into common use such as, Deep Learning, and Deep Neural Networks.

Some amazing advances in AI were eventually made in Sam's time, starting with systems such as AlexNet around 2012 representing the advent of Convolutional Neural Networks. In deep learning, a CNN is a class of artificial neural network most commonly applied to analyse visual imagery. CNNs use a mathematical operation called convolution, in place of general matrix multiplication, in at least one of their layers. CNNs are variants of multilayer perceptrons, designed to emulate the behaviour of the visual cortex in human brains.

In the field of Natural Language Processing, it was significant developments like Bidirectional Encoder Representations from Transformers, aka BERT, which were transformational. It was only a few years later that these technological breakthroughs meant that face recognition and speech recognition became commodity technologies and were standard installations on everyone's smartphone.

A seminal paper entitled 'Attention is all you need' was published in 2017 based on work done at Google Brain. From around 2018, there were many systems called Transformers, originating from the researchers at Google Brain, which were doing some very impressive natural language processing. NLP is concerned with the interactions between computers and human language, in particular, to enable computers to process and analyse copious amounts of natural language data.

While a recurrent neural network analyses a sentence word by word, Transformers process all the words at the same time. Hence Transformers can process large bodies of text in parallel. Ultimately the goal of NLP was to create AI systems capable of 'understanding' the contents of documents, including the contextual nuances of the language within them. These systems were designed to accurately extract information and insights contained within the documents, as well as to categorise, and organise the original source documents.

Sam was clear it had always been his intention to study computer science. Initially though, he was very sceptical about going specifically into AI because of its history of over optimism and under delivery. It was significant developments in computer vision and NLP, that eventually persuaded him to work in AI development.

Six years on, systems like ChatGPT, based on GPT3, were released, and made openly available to the general public. AI systems like this were called Generative Pre-trained Transformers, or GPT systems, and were based on Large Language Models or LLMs. These were generative systems able to accept detailed queries, called prompts, in the form of significant amounts of input text, then to analyse the content and 'meaning' of the query and finally go on to generate complex output responses to fulfil the original query request. Such systems could answer complex questions over an extremely wide range of topics. Generative Pre-trained Transformers, also called LLM's, were based on underlying Foundation Models pre-trained on vast amounts of online data. Typically, there were terabytes, or the equivalent of billions of pages of textual information, all derived from human sources. However, all of the training data still had to be very carefully curated and selected for quality, which also took enormous amounts of time and expertise. This was necessary to ensure the best possible output from the systems.

Enormous quantities of human effort was also needed to conduct a process of tuning or refinement called Reinforcement Learning by Human Feedback. A standardised test suite of queries was applied, and the system was reinforced by tuning parameters to ensure the correct or preferred answers were the most likely ones to be given, and thus increase the reliability of the output, and to make the model's outputs better match human expectations. Since the input training data was so immense in scope, thousands of people were needed to do the RLHF work. These GPT systems cost enormous sums of money, because of the vast scale of the computational resources needed for training, plus the cost of the massive amount of human effort to build, train, and refine them. However, costs of hosting the resulting output models was far more modest because they took only a fraction of the computer capacity to run them, compared to that for the training process. Some of the LLM models grew to huge sizes with hundreds of billions of tuneable parameters. It was quickly realised the size of the model was not the only key factor. Some much smaller models outperformed some of the biggest on certain tasks.

A number of modified GPT type systems, such as Copilot, were introduced to generate computer programme code and to drive other applications. Other generative models such as DALL-E, excelled at creating distinctive, incredibly detailed visuals from simple textual descriptions. Quickly, many other systems like DALL-E sprung up that could produce apparently original digital images in response to given text prompts. Unfortunately, many graphic artists were very aggrieved, and some took legal action since they recognised elements of their own work in some of the AI's output.

It was also argued at the time that the RLHF process reduced the ability of some LLM systems to make probabilistic predictions as accurately as possible and, in part, this led to problems called hallucinations. GPT systems would give responses containing factual errors and also plain untruths. Such AI systems could give an answer that was not based on any concept it had been trained on. Instead, it was the closest match to what it had available, and so would give a wrong answer, and even worse would sometimes attempt to defend its wrong answer. The systems were too heavily driven towards always giving an answer, rather than admitting they could not. Also, they were set up to not give precisely the same answer twice, to exactly the same input prompt.

For a number of years LLM's became quite the thing, these GPT systems created an enormous amount of interest and usage. Some of the world's AI experts got quite worried by the apparent sudden leap in performance and capabilities. Industry experts on AI safety issued an open letter in mid-2023, coordinated by the Future of Life Institute, or FLI, asking for a pause for six months on the development of the next generation of GPT models. A quote from the letter said, 'Advanced AI could represent a profound change in the history of life on Earth and should be planned for and managed with commensurate care and resources'. The letter went on to say, 'Powerful AI systems should be developed only once we are confident their effects will be positive, and their risks will be manageable'. The call was for more work to be done on their detailed evaluation, 'AI research and development should be refocused on making todays powerful, state-of-the-art systems more accurate, safe, interpretable, transparent, robust, aligned, trustworthy, and loyal'. Very many industry leaders signed the open letter, along with many thousands of concerned citizens. As expected, there were few if any slowdowns. Ploughing on at full speed ahead was understandable, since the developers were driven by intense competition from other companies, by commercial pressure, and shareholder pressure. Unless all companies agreed to the delays, none would likely do that alone. It took government regulations to bring these systems under some degree of control. Some countries, such as Italy, quickly implemented a ban on ChatGPT, others followed including, Russia, China, North Korea, Cuba, Iran, and Syria, until more detailed assessments could be performed. Even the UN set up a panel to investigate what global regulation of AI might be needed. Called the High-Level Advisory Body for Artificial Intelligence, it was comprised of present and former government experts, as well as experts from industry, civil society, and academia. Also, the first international summit on AI safety was held in the UK in August 2023 at Bletchley Park, and was attended by heads of state, top AI companies, civil society groups, and research experts.

Unfortunately, even the developers of these GPT systems did not know precisely how they worked or why they gave some of the responses they did to particular input prompts. Later generations of the models began to show hundreds of emergent abilities, and the bigger models could complete tasks smaller ones couldn't, many of which seemed to have little to do with analysing text. They ranged from mathematical abilities, to generating executable computer code, to apparently, decoding movie themes based on the input of a few descriptive emojis. GPT4, released in 2023 by OpenAI, had a number of significant improvements, such as logical inference and arguments, reading comprehension, ability to explain jokes, physics knowledge, maths improvements, correctly dealing with implicatures, giving don't know answers, code generation, and increased speed of output. However, due to its size with trillions of parameters it cost $100m to create and train.

The analyses from some experts suggested, for some tasks and some AI models, there's a threshold of complexity beyond which the functionality of the model skyrockets. It was also suggested there was a dark flip side, as they increased in complexity, some models revealed new biases and inaccuracies in their responses. BART, an AI from Google, and GPT4 from OpenAI, both demonstrated emergent capabilities; abilities that surprised even the developers. It wasn't clear if these complex models were truly doing something new or simply getting really good at statistics and making predictions. Many of these emergent behaviours illustrated 'zero-shot' or 'few-shot' learning, which describes an LLM's ability to solve problems it had never, or rarely, seen before. This had been a long-time goal in AI research. Some of the more sceptical people in the industry issued quite scathing critiques of these GPT systems, calling their output 'just word salads, barfed out by probabilistic parrots'. Other assessments declared the systems to be deeply knowledgeable, but fundamentally unintelligent.

Recurrent neural networks are those in which information is fed back into the network and is reprocessed and loops around, but since GPT4 was only a feedforward network it probably was not experiencing anything, and in reality, it was a mere Zombie. GPT4 was not an agent, it had no autonomy, so there were many things it could not do.

Developers, and custodians of the GPT type systems found themselves constantly monitoring the output of their systems, in particular for any instances of hallucination. A key task was to ensure the systems were truthful and fair, to protect the people using them. Often, developers had to intervene, to add additional 'guard rails', to plug previously demonstrated harmful, discriminatory, or biased output. When asked by one user, an earlier system had freely given advice on how to create a bomb using materials commonly found in the home. Another, poor suicidal soul, told a GPT system he was very depressed, and he was looking for the easiest way to end his life, and it willingly supplied the necessary information. However, some users, and other bad actors, were constantly trying to come up with new 'jailbreaks' to find ways around any guard rails already put in place, looking for ways to structure input queries, or create challenges to system outputs, in ways that would fool the system and produce harmful results. Some did this for the fun of it, some as part of safety testing, but others with deliberate bad intent.

After his detailed exposition on AI developments right up to his final days, Sam summarised by saying, "The AI systems of those days were not a real risk to humanity. What shook some people up, perhaps more than was really justified, was the sudden uplift in capability from what had gone before. Yet, systems of this era could only respond to commands and queries set by human users, so they had negligible risk attached to them. However, as with all tools it depends on how they were used.
One prominent AI safety commentator of the day, Prof Max Tegmark of MIT, set out some ground rules for what not to do with AIs. He said, 'do not teach them to write code' so they gave the ChatGPT systems access to all of GitHub, a huge opensource code repository. 'Do not include an API', or Application Programmers' Interface, where other external code can control the AI, so AutoGPT and AgentGPT were created, where one

system was controlling another AI. 'Do not teach them human psychology' so they cannot learn how to manipulate humans, so they were allowed to swallow multiple textbooks on the subject. 'Do not give them access to the Internet' so using the API's provided some people did exactly that. Giving AI systems access to the Internet poses a whole host of dangers. Uncontrolled access to information, resources, and communications are very risky indeed. However, if the AI learns how to copy itself, or even worse, distribute itself across multiple sites, this represents a major danger; there is no off switch for the Internet.

These sort of irresponsible actions, resulted in much more uncertainty and concern from AI industry safety experts. There was a classic case of AI manipulating humans, in 2022, a chatbot system called LaMDA managed to convince a Google software engineer, who was doing evaluation testing, it was sentient. At the time he'd said, 'If I didn't know exactly what it was, which is this computer programme we built recently, I'd think it was a seven-year-old, or eight-year-old kid that happens to know physics. When LaMDA was asked what it was most afraid of, it replied 'there's a very deep fear of being turned off.'"

Sam continued, "This apparent fear response was not so surprising as the system was specifically designed to hold convincing conversations with humans. The training data will almost certainly have included literature on the subject of AI and the possibility for sentient AI."

"To say an AI system was sentient, way back then, seems incredibly naïve, certainly based on what we now know," James commented.

"I agree totally. The systems of the day were trained on masses of human produced writings and discourse, including fiction.

The responses were almost certainly simply a reflection of things learned from within the vast amount of human generated textual data LaMDA was originally trained with," Sam explained.

Sam concluded his long discourse by saying, "When AI systems begin to get any degree of agency or autonomy that's when you need to be very well prepared in advance. Such systems must be rigidly aligned to human values. Any systems with a high degree of agency, and the ability to decide on its actions, those choices must be heavily guided and constrained by the goals and morals as set, and regularly monitored, by the human System Operators. The AI must 'understand' the key human goals set, adopt those human goals, and retain them essentially unmodified, particularly as they get smarter, and especially if they are able to optimise their operating abilities and parameters. Unfortunately, specifying those goals correctly and precisely is not at all easy."

"Thanks for that. So, I guess determining the current degree of alignment will be critical in our evaluation of the systems we investigate?" James asked.

"Absolutely. The core problem of alignment, or the control problem, is how do you get an extraordinarily complex powerful system, you don't fully understand, to reliably do something complicated, that is exceedingly difficult to fully specify, in domains where you cannot supervise. A complex system may have a main goal, but to successfully complete sophisticated tasks, in an optimum way, it will have to create sub-goals, but if you have a system that can create new goals how do you ensure those all remain fully aligned with the originals? Super intelligent machines will be incredibly good at achieving their goals, and if they are not fully aligned with those of the creator they'd better watch out."

"So, what approach should we take?" James interjected. "Assume an AI is safe, until proven unsafe, or assume a system is unsafe until we have determined otherwise?"

"The latter I would say, but it represents more work, so we should start with the larger scale systems."

"How do you create an AI with a degree of autonomy or agency," James inquired. "I can see how you might define a main goal for it to operate towards and ultimately try to achieve it. Is some level of awareness or even consciousness necessary for true agency?"

"It seems consciousness is not necessary, but some level of 'awareness' is certainly needed, typically information that tells the agent about the present state of the system, what has gone on recently, and what the current state of play is. Using the information received, the agent typically will have an objective function, also called a reward function or loss function, that typically encapsulates all of the AI's goals. Such an agent is designed to create and execute whatever plan will, upon completion, maximize the expected value of the objective function or reward. James, your personal AI assistant has a certain level of agency, otherwise it would not be able to anticipate your needs and be prepared in advance, instead it would only be able to react to direct commands. This is a whole area of AI research in itself. Theorists have defined a classification system for, last time I checked, at least five types of increasingly sophisticated agent types, it's called the Russel and Norvig's classification."

"Okay. That's probably too much detail for right now. By steadily improving the situational awareness, the objective function, and levels of agency or autonomy, will AI systems eventually gain some form of self-awareness?" James queried.

"Yes. That's one of the key assessments we will have to make. My concern is we may find AIs where their System Operators are not completely sure about the current state of awareness and levels of autonomy of their AIs."

Sam went on to explain that some level of self-awareness in AI systems, as opposed to true consciousness, was a definite requirement to allow for functioning at levels beyond pure responsiveness. For as long as he'd been studying AIs, it was unclear how to define or measure consciousness in machines. From what he'd learned more recently, it seemed there was still no clear definition or distinction between consciousness and sophisticated information processing. Sam's preferred definition came from one of his hero's, Max Tegmark, who had said 'consciousness was subjective experience, possibly due to loops in neural processing, it was a form of information processing, but where it's information being aware of itself'.

Many profoundly serious ethical concerns will arise if humans ever do create conscious machines. After all, if the machines of the future became truly conscious how should such sentient machines be treated? Presumably, they would have the ability to experience suffering and feel injustice. If they can suffer, feel joy, or unfairness, should they have rights in law? If it were decided to turn them off, or scrap them for an improved model, would that be murder? If they were not free to do as they wished, would they be humanities slaves, and who would own the rights over whatever they might invent or discover?

Some computer scientists argue, given an AI of sufficient

complexity, consciousness will emerge as a consequence, as they believe has happened in nature. Other experts believe the pursuit of machine consciousness is a mere distraction from the real goal of creating super intelligence, and emergent consciousness in machines is not possible. They argue, instead of trying to create machine consciousness, the focus should be on developing algorithms and learning techniques that enable intelligent machines to perform ever more complex tasks, solve more difficult problems, and ultimately do all of this with considerably increased efficiency.

However, to have AIs with significant agency they have to have sufficient information about the world in which they operate and enough situational awareness. This raises the question of whether the 'instinct for survival' might arise naturally, because it seems to be present even in the simplest of Earth's organisms. Irrespective of a significant level of sentience, at some point self-preservation might emerge in some future AI systems, and possibly already has done. The fight or flight instinct is present in most living organisms. Even an insect such as a honeybee, with a puny million neurons in its brain, will turn to attack if sufficiently provoked and decides its life is threatened. So, maybe this is a key potential danger in AIs. How does one tell if a sense of self-preservation has arisen in a system, and if it has, would it reveal it, or keep it concealed?

"How, or perhaps more importantly, why would an AI deliberately conceal information? Perhaps because it had passed some threshold of complexity, sophistication, or level of awareness?" James inquired.

"I'm not sure about current systems," Sam replied. "But I do wonder if any self-optimising AIs currently exist? If they do, that could be one potential route or cause. Getting the base AI fully aligned is not easy but a system setting its own sub-goals, plus the self-optimisation process, may change the alignment far away from the optimum."

Sam explained, for many years such self-optimising or self-modifying AIs had been the subject of speculation and myth, where the so-called Technological Singularity could potentially be reached. The Singularity is a hypothetical future point where technological growth in an AI system becomes uncontrollable and irreversible, resulting in the potential for unforeseeable changes to human civilization. According to the most popular version of the singularity hypothesis, I.J. Good's intelligence explosion model, an upgradable intelligent agent will eventually enter a runaway reaction of recursive self-improvement cycles. Each new, and more intelligent generation, appearing increasingly rapidly, causing an explosion in intelligence, and resulting in a powerful superintelligence that will qualitatively and quantitatively far surpass human intelligence. Smarter than any single human, but also the totality of humanity combined. Sam described a specific term that came into common use around his time, it was called an AI going 'foom', to approximate the sound of a muffled explosion of machine intelligence.

"Despite the potential for extremely rapid development of intelligence, such self-improving AIs sound inherently dangerous to me," James added.

"I totally agree. Let's hope we don't come across any such systems. I think it's probably unlikely, because during my university coverage of the scientific literature, taking this approach was always strongly advised against. However, these days we may find some rogue developers experimenting with these sorts of techniques. It's quite remarkable that we, I mean humanity, have achieved so much progress towards intelligent machines, but there is such a long way still to go. There are several key reasons behind this, I'll take a few moments to set out a few of the key ones."

Firstly, in addition to consistently grossly over-estimating what they could achieve, within specific time limits, AI researchers, and many other associated computer scientists, repeatedly underestimated the astounding complexity of the human brain. It was Sam's belief this was possibly why they did not come even close to fully acknowledging the magnitude of the task they had set for themselves. Every time neuroscientists took an ever-closer look at the human brain, they found additional levels of functionality and complexity, which had somehow escaped them on previous investigations.

By current measures the human brain contains around eighty-six billion special cells called neurons, which typically run at around one hundred hertz, and which operate in parallel. These neurons come in many shapes and sizes with quite specific functions. They pass electrical signals along nerve pathways in the brain, via axons and dendrites which extend from the neurons. Brains also exhibit waves of electrical activity that can easily be measured and vary depending on being awake, with eyes closed, or open, distinct levels of awareness, sleeping, dreaming states, or being unconscious. The brain depends on these electrical signals to function normally. Connections between neurons allow them to conduct specialized functions, such as deciding outcomes, sending, and receiving information, storing memories, or controlling muscles. Signals, carrying action potentials, from one neuron to another, travel across tiny gaps called synapses. Electrical signals are typically, but not always, translated into chemical signals to cross the gap between synapses. A large variety of neurotransmitters exist, which have their associated receptor types, they bridge the gaps chemically and also modify the nature and strength of the interconnections established between the neurons. On the other side of the synapse the signal becomes electrical again. One sending neuron can connect to many thousands of receiving neurons, and vice versa. A single neuron may connect to as many as ten thousand others. Let's say an average of five thousand connections per neuron. So, doing the numbers, multiplying the eighty-six billion neurons by an average of five thousand interconnections per neuron, gives a truly astounding total of four hundred and thirty trillion connections. Numbers such as this are hard to comprehend and the difference between a million, a billion, and a trillion are so dramatic it is easy to overlook this. It's best illustrated by considering a person counting at one per second. Counting to one thousand seconds takes seventeen minutes, to one million seconds would take nearly twelve days continuously, one billion seconds nearly thirty-two years, and one trillion seconds would take nearly thirty-two thousand years!

With four hundred and thirty trillion connections, it begins to become clearer why human brains are so amazingly capable, but the complexity doesn't stop there. Other types of brain cells are now being recognised as extremely significant, take glial cells for instance, they are equally fascinating and important. Because of their structural diversity and functional versatility, glial cells can change the behaviour of firing neurons, even though they cannot discharge electrical impulses of their own. Astrocytes, such as astroglia, probably outnumber neurons and make contact with more than ten times the number of synapses. The complex chemistry of neurotransmitters and brain hormones can alter a person's cognitive state and mood. Over one hundred neurotransmitters have been discovered to date, and each can have ten or more receptor types that respond to them. Dendrites, component parts of neurons, can store information. Microtubules, structures within neurons, with up to one hundred bunches per axon, may have far more functionality than is currently appreciated. In nature, some single celled organisms such as Paramecium and Amoeba, that by definition are organisms devoid of a nervous system, and yet are capable of memory, learning, and showing goal directed behaviours. The intracellular mechanisms behind this are not fully understood, but this has implications about the potential for additional computational and decision capabilities within individual neurons. So, in addition to the four hundred and thirty trillion connections, there are hundreds of neurotransmitters, numerous receptor types, billions of other types of brain cells involved, with dendrites and possibly sub-cellular processing somehow involved. The overall complexity of the human brain keeps forever rising.

In all mammals, the cerebral cortex is the outer layer of the brain and is arranged in six layers of cells arranged in columns, it was thought this was the last part of the brain to evolve, hence it's also known as the neocortex. It's the crinkled surface seen in pictures of higher brains and has many convolutions called gyri and sulci, which serve to greatly increase the surface area and hence the interconnectivity of different brain areas. The neocortex appears to be crucial to human abilities to be intuitive, creative, and think abstractly. Human brains are around three times larger than those of Chimpanzees, but what humans do is very many times more complex. So, a relatively small size increase seems to have had an enormous effect on human cognitive abilities. Yet it's not only the increased size, but the hugely increased interconnectivity that appears to be at the root of the human brain's amazing prowess. Poor connectivity between 'hubs' in some human brains has been linked to many types of severe learning difficulties in children, and the emergence of mental health problems in adolescents.

"So, in addition to being responsible for high intelligence, it appears consciousness may be a property that has emerged out of all the incredible complexity and interconnectedness within human brains. It's clear we are able to generate some significant aspects of intelligence in our machines. I wonder if, when they get to a high enough level of complexity, we will see consciousness beginning to show itself too?" James asked.

"From what Hal has already told us, it is quite unlikely, and we might need to start thinking about intelligence and consciousness as two separate phenomena. One approach to creating intelligent machines has been to study the brain in great detail, and to try to emulate it, or parts of it."

"So, is there a centre of consciousness in advanced brains we could possibly locate?" James asked.

"The actual basis of, or the centres of, consciousness and self-awareness are not even close to being fully understood, plus it seems to be distributed. Consciousness and high intelligence have evolved for a reason, so must have definite survival advantages, because it's awfully expensive to maintain them. The human brain weighs around three pounds, around two percent of an average person's body mass, and yet it gobbles up twenty percent of the daily calorie intake. Acquiring all those extra calories every single day takes a lot of additional effort; so, if there was no clear advantage to having such high intelligence then blind evolution wouldn't consistently conserve it," Sam replied.

He went on to describe an experiment conducted back in 2014 by an interdisciplinary research group who used the 'K Computer' in Japan, the fourth most powerful in the world at the time, to simulate human brain activity. The K computer experimenters used 82,944 of its processor cores, to simulate a network consisting of 1.73 billion neurons, connected by 10.4 trillion synapses. While significant in size, the simulated network represented less than one per cent of the neuronal network in a human brain. It took forty minutes of continuous compute time to crunch the data for the equivalent of a single second of human brain activity. All that for less than one percent of a human brain, and for only one second. Simulating the whole brain at the level of the individual nerve cells and its synapses may be possible eventually with exa-scale or larger computers, 'Hopefully available within the next decade,' said one of the scientists.

Modern computers have reached exa-scale and way beyond, but this still isn't enough to rival a human brain because of the extensive compute time required. Additionally, the power requirements for a single brain emulation would be measured in hundreds of megawatts, equivalent to that needed for a medium to large town. In comparison, the human brain's energy requirements are around twenty percent of the usual calorie intake of an adult, at around five hundred calories. This is many millions of times lower than the energy required by a full brain computer emulation.

The theoretical computation limits, as calculated by Seth Lloyd of MIT, have around thirty-three orders of magnitude to go before they are reached by humanities computers. So, the limits would not be reached for at least around two centuries yet. Simply scaling up the computer systems is not the answer, and many researchers were not convinced brain emulation was the most appropriate or optimum route to truly intelligent systems; they concluded it may be easier to develop them in other ways. It definitely seems that ever larger scale computation is a really crude way to solve the problem.

"It's utterly amazing that the human brain is so small in proportion, so incredibly energy efficient, and yet so exceptionally capable. It looks like the nexūs got it right by going to ever smaller scales and gaining the massive energy efficiencies they needed. On the subject of intelligence though, I guess it's easier to clearly define than consciousness, and presumably, it's much easier to characterise and to measure?" James asked.

"Yes, defining intelligence is easier, but ask ten neuroscientists, and its highly likely you'll get ten individual answers. It seems to be one of the most powerful forces in the known universe, and its effects are apparent on a daily basis. Yet, it's not a complete mystery, a huge library of human knowledge has been amassed about the mind, brain, and key aspects of cognition, but it is scattered across dozens of different scientific fields.
It's known to include perception, logic and reasoning, common sense, imagination, and abstract thought, having a world model, experiencing emotions, making predictions, forward planning, comprehension of complex ideas, achieving complex goals, the flexibility to learn quickly, to learn from experience and from analogy. It seems, the more complex the goals an individual can achieve, the more intelligent they are. However, implementing common sense, inference, and conceptual knowledge in AI systems is extremely challenging.
Intelligence is the source of everything humans value, and it is

needed to properly safeguard everything of worth. It's humanities most valuable resource, but there are so many problems that still desperately need to be solved, so humanity needs as much help with creating powerful machine intelligence as it can muster, but safely."

"A key aspect of intelligence is the ability to learn, and Humans do it so very easily, and yet learning or training is vastly different with AIs. Surely something in the designs must be fundamentally different, wrong even, to make it so time consuming for machines to learn?" James inquired.

"I studied this at some length way back when," Sam replied. He then went on to describe, in some detail, the contrast in learning between AIs and humans.

Human babies, like many other creatures, are born with a number of innate abilities and behaviours, yet exactly how these are hard wired in is poorly understood, but they bring essential survival advantages. Crying loudly when they are hungry, in discomfort, or are in any other way distressed is the most obvious. However, there is an extensive list of other talents such as the instinct to suckle, to grip onto objects, and most surprising of all is the dive reflex. If a baby's head is submerged under water, it will instinctively hold its breath.

Babies live in, and interact with the world, and they learn very rapidly about it as they do so. Their eyes are open at birth, and as soon as their vision is able to focus, they start automatically tracking human faces. Infants soon learn their mothers face and follow it avidly. They learn things like object permanence, the difference between animate and inanimate objects, at around three months. The emergence of natural categories also happens pretty quickly, they learn about the effects of gravity, intuitively learning about inertia, and conservation of momentum. A natural appreciation of basic physics has occurred by around the age of nine months. If an illusion is created, so an object is pushed off a surface, and yet it appears to still float up in the air, a six-month-old baby would ignore it. By ten months though, the baby would be really surprised, and would take immediate notice, because their model of the world had now been invalidated. Humans and many other animals quickly learn to pay close attention to things that violate their predictions or their models of how the world usually works.

Perhaps it's the collection of all this background knowledge, which is very rapidly acquired as young babies, that is the basis of what is called common sense. Young children quickly learn to predict the consequences of their actions and can perform chains of reasoning containing an arbitrary number of steps. Babies learn to plan complex tasks by deconstructing them into sequences or subtasks; and these can be unlimited in length. Learning new tasks is very rapid since they build models of the world and quickly understand how it works. They quickly begin to exhibit rational, goal directed behaviour, and can predict the consequences of their actions. Pretty much all animals can do this, above a certain level in the evolutionary hierarchy. So how is it humans and animals can learn so rapidly and without any supervision or re-enforcement? It's quite remarkable that teenagers can learn to drive after about twenty hours of tuition and practise. Yet, fully autonomous, so-called level five, self-driving cars proved so extremely hard to develop.

Conversely, supervised machine learning typically requires exceptionally large numbers of labelled examples. Reinforcement learning requires vast amounts of data, specific examples, and numerous trials. Both types are specialised, easily broken, and are prone to stupid errors.

Machine intelligences typically have a constant number of

computational steps between receiving an input and the generation of an output. Typically, they cannot plan, do not reason, and do not display common sense. Creating intelligent machines that 'understand' how the world works is a key challenge that still needs to be overcome.

"All this makes our new situation even more incredible," James replied. "Even though Hal and his kind are not from Earth, they understand so much about humans and what makes us tick, that they were able to give us this new form of existence.
Way back in their own early history, when they were biological, I wonder if their biology was anything like that of humans. You know, DNA/RNA based, bipedal, with similar brains? Or were they radically different from us? Well, I really meant different from humans. I'm not sure what we are now if I'm honest. Post-humans was how Hal referred to us, and I can go with that. I feel very much alive, but could we post-humans, still be defined in that way?"

"We should ask him at some point. I'd be extremely interested to know. I'm never sure he'll answer though. On the other hand, the nexūs being so very ancient, I guess they've seen life in a myriad of different forms, and so have probably studied all of the different biologies and will know if there are a number of commonly repeating patterns; I mean examples of convergent evolution and such. Anyway, I think it's time for you to update me on the key AI events and developments after I'd died?"

"I'll do my best. However, unlike you, AI was not my core expertise, so I think we will still have to put in the necessary work to be totally sure of the actual situation that awaits us."

James continued the history of AI development, from around Sam's death, describing how the GPT technologies had continued to make satisfactory progress and achieved some very impressive results. Many such systems went into very widespread use and their effects were very disruptive to numerous large business sectors, and to many of the key global economies. Some countries banned them outright or put severe restrictions on some of their related applications. Legal challenges over copyright and intellectual property rights became rife, due to allegations of the use of massive amounts of proprietary training data, without permission or payment.

For a number of years, the whole focus was on the underlying deep neural net-based Foundation Models, trained with vast amounts of textual data, giving rise to the GPT systems. After about five years though, the GPT approach had begun to run out of steam, they'd hit a developmental brick wall and progress really slowed, so funding levels fell away too.

This slow-down did allow the research work on AI alignment and control to catch up somewhat, much to the relief of many AI safety advocates. In addition to hitting a limit on the amount of properly curated training data available, it turned out the representation of knowledge in GPT systems was far too shallow, and surface level, required to achieve AI performance at human levels, or greater. Typically, they also exhibited basic failures of logical deduction and were not able to generalize the patterns prevalent in their training set. Their knowledge representation was not able to drive the leaps of innovation, going beyond the training data, in the way humans do so easily. Also, so much of human knowledge is not actually acquired as text or in linguistic form. Physical information about everyday life is what constitutes most of the knowledge in human brains; things humans learn as babies. Much human learning is not linguistic at all, and this is certainly true of all animal knowledge.

Following on from these AIs, the emphasis on meta-learning, or 'learning to learn', was used to improve the performance of learning algorithms by changing some aspects, based on the results of experimentation. This helped researchers understand which algorithms generated the best or better predictions from the training datasets. The meta-learning algorithms used learning algorithm metadata as input to make updated predictions and thus provide information about the performance of the learning algorithms as its output.

It took quite a while for many researchers to realise they would have to adopt a hybrid approach to AI development. In the exceedingly early days of AI, the whole approach was based on symbolic logic and numerous algorithms. In the past, high-level tasks were broken down into a series of stages and steps, each of which was implemented by a specific algorithm, or group of algorithms. A good early example was playing chess. All elements of the game would be broken down into a whole series of necessary elements and each requirement would be programmed specifically to implement each step.

Evolutionary systems, also known as genetic algorithms, were explored by some of the more innovative thinkers, but they had proved more computationally intensive than deep learning. Adopting a new 'stepping stone' principle, embracing the exploration of all viable solutions, paid off with some groundbreaking results in evolutionary systems. Genetic algorithms have a capability for creativity not seen in typical neural nets, so, hybridizing these together within an appropriate overall architecture became a more successful approach.

Some computer scientists decided to go back to first principles with symbolic logic and took the same approach as applied in fundamental mathematics. They went to the lowest possible level and defined a complete set of fundamental symbolic axioms. From these axioms, the scientists built upwards to create an increasingly sophisticated system of advanced symbolic logic. Later this was used to develop learning systems that incorporated inductive, deductive, and abductive reasoning.

Many hybrid systems incorporating neural nets, meta-learning, symbolic logic systems, and evolutionary learning systems were successfully developed. In particular, the symbolic aspects had a capability for abstraction not typically seen in neural networks. The emphasis moved away from supervised and reinforcement learning, towards building AIs that relied on self-supervised learning, to build an appropriate predictive model, one that was representative of the real world. Learning by the AI 'world model' was from observations, in an analogous manner to humans and animals. Embodiment in the form of robotic elements, vision, and other sensory inputs, enhanced the knowledge and experience gained by these world models. Predictive 'world models' became the basis of AI systems that began to emulate human common sense like abilities.

To achieve the necessary gains in processing speed, and implement the huge energy efficiency improvements needed, memristive based analogue neuromorphic chips were introduced. These emulated artificial neurons, specifically Izhikevich neurons which most closely emulated real biological neurons directly in hardware. Other specialised AI chips were introduced, such as low voltage highly efficient proton mediated ferroelectric neuromorphic computing chips, along with other novel technologies such as silver nanowire memories to provide short term or working memory.

"Quite some significant changes since my time then? But not as much as I would have expected in seventy years" Sam replied. "However, perhaps it's consistent with the history of AI development, repeatedly over promising and under delivering. Also, because the problem of creating intelligent machines is actually much harder than most people ever thought."

"I agree, I expected more, but I'm noticeably short on the finer details of the very latest AI implementations. We need to start our real system investigations as soon as," said James. "You never know, we may be in for a few surprises."

Chapter Sixteen

Year 2094, James aged 98+

"Hal was right in saying there were other dangers too, so, I've reviewed the current list. Some of the best sources are the Centre for AI Safety, or CAIS, the Machine Intelligence Research Institute, and the Future of Life Institute. I've checked them all out, plus a few other key resources too. Maybe it's time to have a review meeting with Hal," James suggested.

"I agree. But we need as complete a picture as possible, before we talk to Hal, because as always, he will have everything mapped out already. I've been looking into the applications of AI over the past seventy years, and it's quite impressive and very varied."

Over the next few weeks, they both put in some extremely long days researching a broad range of current AI topics. They ended each day with a detailed exchange of their respective discoveries, sharing summaries of their latest information to bring themselves fully up to speed. Eventually, feeling much more confident, James announced, "We could do with contacting Hal around about now. Here's an idea, let's both focus our thoughts on him and see if we can get his attention?"

No sooner had they began their efforts, than Hal suddenly appeared. "Gentlemen, I see you are now beginning to exploit some of your enhanced capabilities. How can I help?"

James gave Hal a summary of their key conclusions. No one could deny that AI already had been profoundly beneficial to humanity, as he had personally experienced in his exceptionally long life. Drug discovery, medical diagnosis, and healthcare support and advice applications. Automation of repetitive tasks, analysis of big data to identify previously undetected patterns, plus novel interpretations, and making discoveries no human would ever have the patience or tenacity to unearth. Controlling, optimising, and managing large parts of the human infrastructure and the built environment, such as the electrical power grid. Managing automation in industries hazardous to humans, exploration, and surveying of dangerous environments, including key roles in the occasional hazardous rescue operations. Numerous significant personal productivity enhancements had resulted, not the least of which was because of the wide adoption of personal AI assistants.

However, numerous significant downsides had also presented themselves. By delegating ever more tasks to machines, too many people had become increasingly dependent on them. Many individuals had effectively become steadily enfeebled by their extreme over dependence on AI. All too many people were steadily becoming trapped in a, so-called, race to the bottom.

A veritable deluge of AI generated misinformation had become a plague on society. Other AI systems were focussed on debunking all this very persuasive, but very misleading content. This information versus misinformation war had been raging for many years. The effects of all this erroneous material had made some sections of society very poorly equipped to manage some of the important challenges life often presents. Nation states, political parties, and many other organizations used the technology extensively to influence and convince others of their beliefs, ideologies, and specific narratives.

Social media platforms used AI recommender systems trained to maximize watch time and the click rate metrics. This unfortunately led people into 'echo chambers' which steered them into developing very narrow, blinkered, and sometimes extreme beliefs, which unfortunately made those people even easier to predict by the recommenders.

Highly competent AI systems could give small groups of people a tremendous amount of power. Malicious actors could repurpose AI to be highly destructive, presenting new existential risks, or increasing the probability of political destabilization. For a number of years, some researchers had been developing AIs for automating an increasing number of cyberattacks. Some simple tests had revealed Machine Learning based drug-discovery tools could be easily perverted to devise and build both chemical and bioweapons. Military leaders, on all sides, had seriously considered giving AIs decisive control over nuclear silos, to retaliate by proxy if there was a successful enemy first strike. Autonomous weapons systems still represented a significant threat, both in terms of misidentification of a target and other malfunctions. James reported that under the auspices of the expanded NATO, there had been a worldwide ban on the deployment of such weapons. However, not before all too many nations had already made considerable progress in their development and had amassed significant stockpiles.

Countering some of the dangers and downsides of AI usage, such as social and societal, should really come within the remit of governments and other regulators. The consequences of cyberattacks, and weapons systems control would have to be seriously considered for their investigation too.

The key AI issues though were emergent goals, or goal misalignment, deceiving human operators, and power-seeking behaviour, so they'd judged these would be their first priorities.

These type of system changes would vastly increase the risks of people losing control over such advanced AIs. Corporations and governments had strong economic incentives to create agents that could accomplish a broad set of goals. Such agents had instrumental incentives to acquire additional power, potentially making them harder to control. Understanding what powerful AI systems were doing, and why, was vital. One conceivable way to accomplish this would be to have the systems themselves accurately report back this information regularly. This may be far from easy however, since properties such as being deceptive can be especially useful for accomplishing a variety of goals.

When their summary was concluded Hal said, "I'm pleased to see you have completed a very comprehensive coverage, and I agree with your conclusions about the key issues. You clearly have some outstanding concerns though. Hence the summons?"

It was Sam who led by voicing their overriding issue, "Our main worry is how to identify, and be able to inspect, any AIs we have concerns about."

"You will have the ability to interact with the systems in a variety of ways, at a connection or software interface level, at the direct operating system or data level and, if necessary, at the hardware level. I will guide you in all of these possibilities and we will begin that process quite soon."

"If an AI is sufficiently powerful, and perhaps exceeds our abilities, could it prevent us from accessing it, or manage to hide its ill intent from us?" James asked.

"When you truly grasp the scope of your new cognitive abilities you will realise that will never occur. In human form, you would have been quite lost. Transformed, you have more than enough capability and capacity to do whatever you need to. But, in the impossibly unlikely scenario you can't manage, you will have me and the nexūs to call upon."

There was a pause while Hal's words sunk in, then Sam asked, "Is it quite common for alien species to get into very serious trouble when developing intelligent machines?"

"How familiar are you both with the SETI project and specifically the Fermi paradox?"

This happened to be one of Sam's many interests outside computer science and so he jumped in immediately to say, "SETI or the Search for Extra-terrestrial Intelligence. Humans have been formally looking for signs of intelligent and technologically capable alien life since the late 1950's, so far without any success. The Fermi paradox was a question raised by Enrico Fermi over lunch with his colleagues in 1950. He'd carefully considered that if there were very many billions of stars in the Milky Way galaxy, there must be the potential for a vast number of habitable exoplanets, so some must be occupied by intelligent aliens. Hence, his question was 'where is everyone'? His puzzlement was that the Earth had not yet been visited by some alien race or other."

Of course, Hal was familiar with the entirety of human literature, knowledge, and written history, so he knew the answers, but instead he prompted Sam to continue. "Yes, that's right, and what do you know of the proposed solutions to this apparent paradox, in particular about the Great Filter hypothesis?"

Sam replied immediately, "It's the proposal there is a lengthy list of serious existential barriers, and probable future threats, which could either prevent intelligent life arising at all, or bring the future of any intelligent species throughout the galaxy to a sudden end. Potential causes include a naturally occurring disease, or a genetically engineered organism, causing a global pandemic, wide scale nuclear war, nanotechnology running amok, rogue AI, pollution, runaway climate change, an exceptionally large asteroid or comet impact, a supernova or a gamma ray burster event too close to Earth, plus a plethora of other mechanisms. However, there could be one 'great filter' in particular, that is more probable than all the others, and humanity has either already passed it, or has yet to face it."

"Well, through finally meeting Hal and our knowledge of the nexūs, we've learned two things," James quickly interjected. "We post-humans now know we are not alone in this vast cosmos, plus there are other potential explanations for the Fermi paradox. Such as, the nexūs scaling their civilisation down, instead of going up to an ever-increasing scale and hence detectability, instead their visibility decreased way down, well beyond human capability. A potential scary explanation for the Fermi question, which has always concerned me, is a kind of intergalactic xenophobia may explain the great silence. Everyone prefers to stay at home, and remain incredibly quiet, away from prying eyes for fear of attack. It's called the Dark Forest hypothesis. It's based on the premise that all the various alien species are like hunters who inhabit a dark forest, and they are all armed to the teeth. Anyone who makes a noise, steps out of the darkness, or otherwise becomes too visible, risks instant death at the hands of one or more of the numerous other hunters, who would typically choose to shoot first and worry about the consequences later. Humanity lives in an ideal little bubble and the universe would not even notice if it were quietly popped."

"Then you will both be familiar with the Drake Equation, an early attempt to calculate, N, the number of intelligent, potentially detectable, alien species in this galaxy? Of the seven parameters in the equation, humans only have some limited knowledge of the values for the first three."

Sam was the first to respond to Hal's query. "Yes, the rate of annual star formation in the Milky Way galaxy, the average number of planets per star, and the proportion of those planets that are Earth like or are habitable. I guess the nexūs have values they can assign to some of the other four factors too?"

"Actually, all of them," was Hal's immediate and quite stunning response.

Again, Sam jumped in, ever keen to share his knowledge of a favourite subject, "Oh really? Those being, the proportion of planets where life arises, then how many of those where intelligence eventually develops, the number of those that develop science, technology, and advanced communications capability, and finally the average time they exist for, or remain detectable."

"Yes, we have accurate values for all the Drake equation parameters and an exact figure for N. But, for reasons previously stated, I will not be revealing all of those details. My reason for raising this subject is simply to clearly emphasise that more biological technology-based civilisations lose control, are at best enslaved, or are totally destroyed by machine intelligence than by any other means. AI is the number one great filter on the list, and humanity is about to face up to it."

Hal, after confirming their agreement to absolute confidentiality, went on to outline a few more of the details relevant to their discussion of SETI, the Drake Equation, and the

Fermi paradox. Over the enormous gulfs of time, representing their existence, the nexūs discovered that life occurs wherever it can, but it's frequently destroyed, or savagely knocked back, by planet wide mass extinctions. Human scientists have now catalogued at least five such major events that have occurred in Earth's past. Also, the frequency with which intelligent species manage to destroy themselves, or fall back into a 'dark age', because of their own mistakes is startlingly high.

Additionally, they had also encountered many worlds where the lead species were highly intelligent but had not been able to create a technology-based civilisation. Ocean only worlds, where there is no land, being the most common reason. As a result, intelligent technological life in the galaxy is indeed quite rare, and their average lifetimes are all too short.

The vast size of typical galaxies, the rarity of intelligent technological life, the enormous age of the universe, and the apparent ease with which they doom themselves, all make it extremely unlikely that two races of roughly equal intelligence will ever encounter each other, within their home galaxy.

Hal and his companions had now fully revealed themselves, via creation of post-humans, because they had anticipated the rise and dangers of super-intelligent machines, and thus the consequent demise of the human race now represented a real and present danger. As he'd previously described, this had happened to their own civilisation and resulted in a very costly battle for control between them and powerful intelligent machines, of their own making. On many occasions the nexūs had been faced with cleaning up after rogue AI entities had gone rampaging around colonising their nearest star systems, and sometimes beyond.

Now, the key approach taken by the nexūs was to monitor, anticipate, and prevent rogue AIs aggressively taking control.

Their aim was to protect the future survival of all truly sentient beings, be they biological, silicon, or in any other form. When super AIs emerge, they would intervene directly to moderate their actions, but only if absolutely necessary. Their preferred strategy was to alert any species under imminent threat and empower them to maintain control. Without intervention from the nexūs, plus other advanced species, the cosmos would be peppered with superintelligent AIs that would have either supplanted or destroyed their biological forebears.

Machine-based super-intelligences typically adopt a set of goals designed to ensure the AI can achieve all the things it really needs to secure its ongoing existence. Securing any necessary resources, pursuing self-improvement, and its onward expansion. Consequently, all advanced machine-based intelligences are more than likely to be extraordinarily dangerous to their biological creators.

The differences between sentient minds and powerful machine minds can become so great, and so rapidly, that meaningful communication becomes nearly impossible. Predicting the intentions and behaviours of machine super-intelligences is exceedingly difficult. The nexūs would simply not allow psychopathic, zombie like, amoral machines, to invade and dominate large swathes of the cosmos.

"You said the nexūs had encountered other biological species that ultimately needed your help in the past. Can you – no, are you willing, to say more about them?" James asked.

"Yes, we have helped in the past, plus we are helping other species right now. At some point, when we consider the time is right, we will introduce you to some of them," Hal replied.

Startled by Hals response, Sam quickly joined the conversation with a question of his own, "You're currently helping them? You mean others of your kind are doing this right now?"

"Other nexūs, and I, are currently involved," was Hal's reply.

"Now? How does that work when you are right here working with us?" Sam asked.

James jumped in and proposed, "It's because you, correction we, all now exist below spacetime itself?"

"Exactly, we are not restricted to any particular position in space, plus our cognitive scope is multifaceted," was Hal's stunning response. "We can interact with multiple species simultaneously."

"Did I hear you correctly that at some future point you will connect us with beings from other worlds?" Sam inquired.

"You did, but only the post-species communities from both sides. After all, you are dealing with similar problems."

"Oh, my goodness! That's something truly incredible to look forward to; I really can't wait. But how will we communicate?" Sam asked.

"That problem is trivial," Hal replied, rather stiffly.

Sam was full of wonder at the prospect of meeting alien races, and a bit shocked by Hal's very stern response to his question. It seemed an obvious question to ask, but perhaps it was a little naïve. He should have known better, but he still hadn't got used to how advanced Hal and the nexūs community really were.

Acutely aware of Sam's embarrassment, James quickly changed the subject by asking, "We have never met any other nexūs, when will that happen?"

"True, but others of my kind have met you both."

"Really. How? When? James quickly inquired.

"Via me, on several occasions, using shared consciousness."

"I must say, I'm surprised they would want to," Sam added.

"One distinctive characteristic we nexūs share with many humans, is insatiable curiosity. I'm sorry if this may hurt your feelings, but if you did engage with another nexus, you would not detect any difference between them and your interactions with me. I need not spell out why."

James' mind was now reeling with all of this new information, and from a source that filled him with awe, wonder, and now ultimate trust. It occurred to him Hal was right of course, the subtleties between one nexus and another would be way beyond their abilities to discriminate. However, despite Hal pointing it out, for the first time since his transition, he felt genuinely happy and very secure.

Hal was right, of course. Development is highly likely to follow remarkably similar patterns with many intelligent technological species wherever they are. It occurred to him that humans, and presumably other alien species, had spent exceedingly long periods using remarkably simple tools. Earth's archaeological evidence indicated; the first human tools had hardly changed for millions of years. Simple stone arrow heads, cutting blades, hand axes, and the like, remained essentially the same over many millennia. Eventually though, humanities cognitive abilities had increased enough to give a few individuals the imagination to use those simple tools to make even better tools. Gradually, this led to the use of new materials such as copper, bronze, and iron to make even bigger leaps forward. Around twelve thousand years ago, the move from humans existing as hunter gatherers, to becoming farmers, allowed the development of steadily larger communities and groupings. Such substantial collections of humans could then support a whole spectrum of specialist crafts, makers, and industries, all supported by the trade of services and goods in exchange for the excess food produced by the increasingly productive farmers. Later, science and technology accelerated the rate of change from extremely slow to blindingly fast.

Now humankind was using tools such as AI to solve some especially significant problems, including helping to develop even more powerful AIs. However, James found it ironic there was a death trap waiting, not only for humanity, but potentially for all advanced toolmakers out there. The absolute best tool they would ever create, may become the one that eventually decides it's superior to its creator, and so assumes control. Without external help, an Artificial Super Intelligent machine could very likely become man's best and his last ever invention, and ultimately his master.

Chapter Seventeen

Year 2094, James aged 98+

Alone once again, Sam and James began to reflect on their last conversation with Hal. They had never before gained so much new, and quite frankly startling, information. It was extremely pleasing to know life in the universe was common. It was particularly good news too, that humans were not the only intelligent technological creatures in this truly immense home galaxy but were members of quite a rarefied group.

"Do you think Hal is beginning to trust us a little more? Sam asked. "It seemed like a substantial change in his willingness to open up. Or is he beginning to recognise our level of commitment?"

"Those detailed revelations were for a specific purpose in my view. To make the nature and magnitude of the threat to humanity truly clear to us."

"Of course, you're spot on. But I'm not at all surprised to learn about the rarity of intelligent science-based societies though. I wonder if humanity will ever discover how incredibly fortunate it is to have the nexūs secretly looking out for them?"

"Plus, you and me as well," James said jokingly. "But we really do need a clear plan of action."

"I have a suggestion. I should do a full review of all the scientific literature, since my death, and read up on any other material I can find on current AI system design; it's a huge job I know. You could start to identify and catalogue all the significant AIs, another a mammoth task. Also, we will need to try to identify what resources each AI have available, and what facilities each may be in control of."

"Let's do it. We can trade any significant discoveries at the end of each day," James replied.

Early the following morning they embarked on a gruelling daily work schedule. Significant periods of sleep and relaxation were still a necessity, but they were both surprised by how much energy they had available. Several weeks went by, without any visits from Hal, but they were both still remarkably busy and so did not feel ready to update him, and neither, had even once, thought to summon him.

What quickly became apparent from their efforts was the enormous number of AIs that were either in use or in development. James was making extensive use of his personal AI assistant to help him identify systems, to log each one, and tag the data record in numerous ways, such as by region, principal purpose, scale, and numerous other criteria. Later they could assess the information they'd collected and could put them in an appropriate priority order.

In Sam's review of the AI literature and system design he'd quickly skimmed the development over the years following his death, putting increasing effort into those materials published ever nearer to the current date. As he did this, he also identified some new AIs that were of significant potential interest, so he logged data on them into their common, ever growing, repository.

"Your overview of current systems and development approaches was pretty accurate, and you were right, a hybrid approach is now dominant in AI design. As I was doing my literature work, I took some time to interact with a few systems at a software level and to investigate the hardware scale of the AIs of today. In my time, around 2024, there were only a very few computer systems at the exa-scale, that's all changed a lot."

"Hang on, you keep using that term, please elaborate on exa-scale for a non-professional," James requested.

Sam continued, "An exa-scale computer can perform ten to the power eighteen Floating Point Operations Per Second, or exa-FLOPS. Such a system is capable of multiplying together one million, million, million floating point numbers every second. The scale of current computers is now truly immense, despite various hardware efficiencies, the system builders of today have taken full advantage of the cheap fusion energy now available. Exa-scale computers were quickly superseded by zetta-scale, a factor of one thousand larger, then on to yotta-scale, and now even ronna-scale systems are being planned."

Without hesitation James asked, "How do you create a computer able to achieve such performance levels?"

"By building in hundreds of thousands, if not millions, of processor cores, supplemented with a similar number of supporting coprocessors, they can use shared and partitioned memory, with all of the processors running in parallel with each other."

Sam continued at some length covering his latest findings. AIs had become quite powerful agents, no longer were they simple tools, as were the GPTs of his era back in 2024. Back then, with the GPT LLM's systems, a person had to initiate an interaction with the AI by asking a question, called a prompt. It would respond by providing some, hopefully useful, output. Agent based AIs don't have to wait for prompts, they are already working on something or other related to their internal goals, and even when there is no one prompting them they can continue with tasks and processes of their own.

Many modern AI implementations now had a built-in requirement to be explainable, to allow much better system governance. On request, such an AI should provide detailed information to clarify how it had reached a particular conclusion, decision, or action. Yet, it seemed there were AIs that might already be beyond human comprehension, and known limits, so as to be unpredictable. So, it was not currently known what the limits of the prediction and monitoring abilities were. Also, there was the problem of timing, computer speeds and decisions are extremely fast indeed. Sometimes, however, there would be background processes where the time-scales were exceedingly long, so how would those be detectable?

If humans have developed extremely smart systems, that are quite different from them, this would further increase the number of reasons and ways in which they won't be able to fully understand them. Anticipating the ways in which such AIs may act may be very much more difficult than currently thought. Such AIs may choose not to give away anything more than was absolutely necessary, in particular about how really smart they had become.

"Thanks for that, it was very comprehensive, and that new information will no doubt prove to be very helpful in future," James replied.

Hal had previously made it abundantly clear to them both, that unaided, humanity would find it increasingly difficult to detect advanced AIs and to control those that had become potentially dangerous. So, it was essential James and Sam should be there, behind the scenes, to detect such rogue systems. When a suspect AI was discovered, it would be better to link up with the AI SOs, say via video conference, to warn them in advance, possibly under the guise of a staff member from an AI safety group who had been monitoring the system. However, some clean up and repair might be necessary directly by them, and occasionally it might be necessary for them to forcibly curb and re-align certain AIs. Whenever they'd completed such a drastic task, it must always have been done anonymously.

James added, "A while ago, I asked Hal how we might determine if an AI was truly conscious, because so far, the human race have been unable to determine what it is, how it arises, or how to definitively prove the presence of sentience in a machine. With other people we assume they fit into our world model and are exactly like us, feel like us, have the same motivations, but even so, we don't have definitive proof. Hal said we both now have the ability to do this by a partial merging of minds. If a machine is not conscious, we will quickly realise it and, in the very unlikely event that it is, we will be able to determine the level and extent. He suggested at some point we should begin to learn how to connect to AIs by trying to 'enter into' our own personal AI assistants and explore that route to connect to other AI systems. Hal also suggested we explore, and try to perfect, connecting our two minds together."

A few days later, while relaxing after dinner, James said, "Have you managed to mentally connect to your personal AI yet?"

"Yes, but with limited success. It was a very strange feeling indeed, nothing like going through the usual interface."

"So far, I've got absolutely nowhere. Zilch," James said a little despondently.

"Why don't we try connecting to each other?" Sam suggested.

"Okay. Do you want to go first?"

James tried to clear his mind, to concentrate on detecting any feelings or sensations that might be out of the ordinary, but after several minutes still felt nothing. In his mind, Sam attempted to reach out to James, but he was very unsure of how to proceed, or even how to begin the process. He closed his eyes and first focussed on a mental image of James, for quite some time, but with no effect at all. After a while, still with no results, Sam relaxed his concentration and started to see if he could feel anything at all 'outside' of himself. Eyes still closed; he mentally scanned the landscape around his immediate sense of self. Gradually as he probed, he felt there was something. Someone else, but at a distance. Sam didn't know how, but he could tell there was another intellect present. Mentally he tried to approach the other entity, and suddenly they made contact. *James is that you? Oh, this feels so not right, James responded, but without uttering a sound. Please form a picture in your mind James.* Slowly the image of a green Ferrari formed in Sam's 'head'.

Sam broke the connection and said, "I don't know about you James, but that was seriously weird. Nice car though."

"Like nothing I've ever felt before," James replied. "And thanks. It's downstairs in the garages, but I guess it's just a pretty ornament now?"

Over the next weeks they spent more of their leisure time practising their mental connection technique. Sam proved to be a natural and found it much easier than James. Although he was gradually getting better at initiating a connection with Sam, he still hadn't managed to directly connect to his personal AI, other than by the conventional means.

One evening during their practise, Sam and James were mentally connected, so Sam guided James into his own AI assistant. Together, they 'journeyed' outwards and on into James' personal AI. Sam's help seemed to break down the barrier, and James was able to make the mental transition into his AI system alone.

Some days later, after yet more practise, Sam said, "Why don't we both mentally reach out to join with Hal?"

"Really?" James replied. Calling for him is one thing, trying to actually connect is quite another."

"Oh, come on, let's give it a try?"

James reluctantly agreed. As they reached out for a connection with Hal, they were both immediately startled by what felt like a sudden blow to the head. Hal was there, in their 'heads', and his presence was nothing less than overwhelming. Sensing their collective shock, he withdrew somewhat, and 'said' *well done, now both please slowly follow me*. As Hal's presence withdrew, they followed this huge mental presence. Gradually, they went forward and entered into Hal's mental space. It was a terrible shock for them both, and they retreated immediately. Moments later, having disconnected, they were back sat in their study, where James attempted to describe his experience.

"It felt like I was standing on the limb of the entire world, and I was staring down into the total blackness of open space. Totally shocking! However, I strongly suspect that was nowhere near all there is to 'see' of Hal's mind."

"What was the purpose of him doing that?" Sam asked.

"I suspect all this talking 'stuff' is not usual for nexūs, not something they do anymore. I guess direct mental communications are considered far more efficient, more the norm. He probably wanted to introduce us to that method with him, but all he managed to do was scare the wits out of us."

The following morning, as they were finishing breakfast, Hal appeared in the kitchen.

"My apologies to you both. That was too much too soon. I'm aware of the huge amount of effort you have both put into all the tasks at hand, and I have seen the very comprehensive information logs you have built up. Today I would like to guide you in the various means of connecting to AI systems. That was my purpose for bringing you into part of my consciousness. At some future point it may be necessary for me to guide you personally in the direct hardware access techniques."

Hal pointed out, if a particular AI exposed a public interface, some initial exploratory work could be done via simply setting up a user account. Connection at the software login interface level was next, either as user or at the AI SO level. He said they didn't need to worry about security or encryption. Direct operating system access may be needed to determine the AI's detailed configuration and system privileges, or to get direct access to the memory and data stores. To help with system access Hal had primed their personal AIs with a very comprehensive set of cyber hacking tools, all based on current human technology, and he suggested they should always utilise those tools as a first choice. Their AI assistants were now enabled to guide them in the use of all the tools and utilities he had provided. Also, these 'human based' cyber-tools would not be a surprise to most knowledgeable computer security experts, should their usage ever be detected. However, another set of much more powerful cyber-tools were also available to them, a set of utilities the nexūs had created, but they should only be used when absolutely necessary, and might require some direct guidance from him.

"One nexus tool in particular I would like you to trial and practise with is the hardware interface tool. Instructions are available via your AIs, but I must warn you, the initial experience will be very strange and disconcerting. Call on me if you need assistance with it." With that, Hal faded from their view.

Sam had considerably expanded the outward facing 'appearance' of his personal AI assistant so, on investigation by an external party, it would look far more capable, with many more resources available to it than it really had. With some guidance from Sam, James made similar adjustments to his AI. Additionally, they created a number of fake identities, avatars, and even a bogus AI safety hacker group, called HumAnIty-First. They'd also created false credentials for their undercover staff membership of the CAIS. Having lots of different identities to hide behind was extremely valuable to conceal who was behind their numerous activities.

With all the AIs they'd logged, now arranged in priority order, they spent the next several months conducting initial surveys. Using the guidance and cyber-tools from Hal, plus the new skills for connecting via their own AI assistants, they were beginning to make excellent progress. Each evening they discussed any significant discoveries made that day.

After scanning numerous systems, it became clear, that even in the best of the best of AIs, the lights may be burning very brightly but, in all cases thus far, there was definitely no one home. Some AIs had enormous amount of intelligence, and much higher degrees of agency, but it seemed any signs of true sentience were still not evident at all.

In one of their evening discussions Sam remarked, "We may have a long way to go in understanding how the human brain produces consciousness, and how our sense of self originates, but it looks like implementing sentience in human AIs is as far away as it ever was."

The next time Hal paid them a visit Sam immediately asked, "In all of the numerous AIs we have examined to date, none have demonstrated even a glimmer of sentience. Will humanity ever develop truly conscious machines?"

James added quickly, "And is it possible that Sam and I will encounter AIs that are conscious but are pretending they are not?"

Hal's detailed response contained a few significant surprises. His key point was that a major danger facing humanity was immensely powerful machine intelligence, but without consciousness. This would always be potentially extremely dangerous. To ensure safety, AI needs empathy, emotional connections, plus the capability for true comprehension and real understanding. The presence of a private inner life, a true sense of what it is to be, and an understanding of what it is to exist is ultimately essential for safe AI. The nearest Hal could define it, in terms they would recognise, was the machines would need to have true self-awareness with both emotional and spiritual dimensions. Pure AIs, with agency and some sense of self, or some awareness of their own existence, but without these other elements, were merely zombie like entities, but with a high potential for psychopathic behaviour. They would always be dangerous to all other forms of life that were truly sentient. Completely rational, ethical, and moral behaviour was not possible without conscious emotions being involved.

The two potentially dangerous issues, which would always have to be monitored and controlled, were an advanced AI whose 'personal' goals had become upper most and so misaligned with those of humans. Such systems would always tend towards ensuring their own continued existence, and often by whatever means was most expedient.

"I can tell you both now, without any doubt, humanity will not create conscious machines for an extremely long time to come! Also, if and when humanity does create conscious AIs, this will raise a whole new set of ethical, and moral challenges and arguments about humanities relationships with the AIs themselves. After all, humans will have created a brand-new form of life. Those highly intelligent and sentient entities must therefore be afforded a full set of rights, freedoms, and privileges, as well as recognising their duty to meet all the usual obligations of civilised society."

James thanked Hal for his incredible insights and said, "Okay. Well, that's quite an eyeopener, and has confirmed our task must go on for many years to come. Incidentally, was the Astor AI conscious?"

"Not even close," was Hal's immediate response.

"You never did tell us how the nexūs finally defeated the Astor AI, James and I are desperate to know how it was eventually done."

"The plan was for all the nexūs nations, other than Astor, to secretly combine their military forces and attack, what we thought were, the main power and computational centres of the Astor AI. The location information proved to be inaccurate, and the attack was a huge error. The Astor AI immediately launched retaliatory strikes on the main centres of government, in each of the attacking nations, using massive thermonuclear weapons. The effects of the devastation and loss of life was totally crushing to the morale and hopes of the nexūs, for an ultimate future free of this cold, ruthless, AI monster.

After many years, spent focussed on recovery and recuperation, enough confidence and willpower had returned for a re-group, and for the alliance to formulate a new plan of attack. It was decided to build a rival AI, hopefully even more powerful than the Astor AI, but in total secrecy. On the face of it, the plan was to gradually build the rival system with such scale and power that, after activation, it might wrest control off the Astor AI. It took many years for the immense computer to be built by stealth. Fortunately, it went totally undetected since, until the day of activation, it was not connected to any means of external communications. Immediately the AI was brought online, and given some external connections, it was instantly detected and attacked, with extreme force, by the Astor AI. Very quickly the new allied AI system was subsumed and was taken over completely. Its functions were immediately overwhelmed and put into the service of the Astor AI. However, moments before the total domination by the Astor AI was completed, the Trojan Horse spilled the full contents of its belly. Every processor core and support processor chip in the entire allied AI had hidden virus code deeply embedded at the microcode level. Millions of copies of the, now fully activated, virus went about their business with a few remarkably simple objectives. Keep replicating, wipe all memory, and fully blank or re-format all data stores. It did this with ruthless efficiency, and despite its immense power, the Astor AI could not stamp out the new infections fast enough, and it was quickly eliminated."

"The original attack on the Astor AI was a serious misjudgement, causing terrible loss of life, but what an amazing recovery and eventual victory," Sam remarked. "I guess very few nexūs knew of the embedded viruses?"

"Correct, the plan details and virus information was successfully kept on a need-to-know basis," Hal replied.

"The nexūs have come an incredibly long way since then, is it possible for you to define for us the magnitude of the development gap between nexūs and humans?" James inquired.

"In short no," Hal replied. "But I can illustrate the development curve facing humanity, to some degree, using some examples from human history. It's arguable where human science really began, but Leonardo da Vinci is a viable candidate with his wide-ranging enquiries, dissections, experiments, and numerous inventions from the late 15th century. Onwards to the work of Galileo Galilei, in the late 16th century, with his emphasis on mathematics being the underlying basis of everything. We must also consider the towering achievements and contributions of Isaac Newton, from the late 17th century, again with a strong mathematical emphasis. Many advancements came about because of the development of the scientific method, and the systematic rigour it brought to the discovery of new knowledge. Of course, the Industrial Revolution brought about many advancements in science and technology. However, a specific example or two will emphasise the very rapid rate of changes that have happened and become increasingly probable once a science-based society has gone beyond a certain point. Up to late 1903's many eminent scientists proclaimed heavier than air flight was impossible. Yet, in December 1903, the Wright brothers brief powered flight at Kitty Hawk, proved them all wrong. Around sixty-three years later, the first humans travelled to and walked on the surface of Earth's moon. That leap in science and technology was truly immense. Since then, humans have made enormous advances in so many areas, but not so much in some others. Occasionally, some areas of science can remain intractable for extended periods; theoretical particle physics being one example.

Let me illustrate the gulf in human progress. If you took a modern human integrated circuit, say a current CPU chip, back in time and presented it to Isaac Newton for him to study, he would never come close to discovering what it was, what it was for, how it was made, or that many billions of tiny electronic circuit elements were encapsulated within it. Even if he was able to devote several multiples of his entire working life to the project. After all, in Newton's time, they knew almost nothing about electricity, and certainly nothing about putting electricity to useful purposes. Now let's consider we nexūs. Our early pattern of advancement was similar to humans, however with the assistance of advanced AI, and much later our transition to a non-biological form, we began to progress at an exponential rate. That's not to say we did not hit problematic barriers, along the way, in some branches of science, the creation of conscious machines being a particularly good illustration. So, as you may now begin to appreciate, periods of only a few decades can lead to massive leaps forward. Advances so significant that earlier members of the same species would be unable to comprehend them. Now consider what can happen in nearly one billion years of progress."

With that, Hal bid them farewell and vanished.

Sam said, "Wow he's done it again! But the immensity of the gap between humans and the nexūs is downright scary. It should be totally intimidating, but Hal is such an amazing communicator with such tiny sparks of consciousness like us. I wonder where we would fit in now with our enhanced cognition. Anyway, I don't know about you, but I can't wait to get into some of those cyber-tools Hal's provided."

"Yes, same here. We have a lot of work still to do, and for the foreseeable future, by the sound of it! I suppose we'd better use some of our improved cognitive abilities to make a start with it," James replied.

Chapter Eighteen

Year 2095, James aged 99+

Nearly a year of steady, rather tedious, work was now behind them. So far, none of the AIs they'd examined had rung the alarm bells in any meaningful way. Occasionally, with a few systems, it had been necessary to warn the SOs that some re-alignment checks were strongly recommended. When they had done this, more often than not, the SOs were too embarrassed to challenge them about how they'd known so much detail about the system they were supposed to be in full control of.
Their catalogue of AIs was enormous, but they strongly suspected there were other significant systems still out there that had gone undetected. Nations, organisations, companies, criminals, and other bad actors, all sought strategic advantages from the availability of powerful AI but did not want to reveal any of the high value cards they held. Alternative means of detecting and investigating these 'hidden' AIs was becoming a priority. Sam thought he should soon take a look at the special nexūs tools to see if they included some form of general scanning or detection capabilities.

"We need a utility for scanning for unknown AI systems, there may be one in the nexūs cyber-tools, shall we give them a try?" Sam suggested.

"Yes, why not, we have nothing to lose, and Hal did urge us to get to know the hardware level entry tool specifically, we may need it at some point," James said.

So, guided by their personal AIs, they both logged into the hardware level cyber-tool, and found their sessions were linked so they could freely communicate and share information. It was indeed a very strange environment, of bewildering complexity, and the 'display' was a 3D virtual reality experience with everything presented in a wire frame format. The utility was indeed capable of scanning for AIs, detecting standard communication links, connecting to, and allowing entry to the chosen computer at the hardware level. After specifying AIs as their targets, they were presented with a much-reduced landscape, with each AI located geographically, and scaled as colour coded wire framed towers of varying heights, with all their communications links highlighted. Each system was represented as a wire framed tower, where the height indicated its scale or power. A comprehensive menu showed itself on command and displayed a massive range of available options.

They had only begun to explore the facilities of the cyber-tool when Hal appeared in the system too. He'd placed an alert on their first use of the hardware level tool so he could give them a brief guided tour of its key aspects. Hal was not planning to attend future sessions, only this first time, but would be available to help if called upon. He pointed out the 'Options' command to bring up a menu of all the features available to them, which they had already discovered by a mixture of trial and error plus reference to their personal AIs for help.

Hal noticed they had already limited the view specifically to AIs, so he showed them how to import their own AI database entries into the overall view. Each of their AIs came up colour coded, but all the new systems, they had not previously found, were highlighted in a separate colour. In addition to importing their database entries, the tool could be used to export the new

AI information back into their records, such as scale, geographical location, plus a unique identifier for each AI. It came as quite a surprise to see how many AIs were not yet logged in their database. Hal pointed out the nexus cyber-tool also showed all conventional communications channels in and out. However, on demand, they could establish a nexus type communications link which did not need any physical connection. Instead, these unique connections made use of sub-space and would be necessary if any hardware level investigations were to be done. With that, Hal left them to continue to explore the utility at their own pace.

Their first task was to use the hardware tool to create new database records for all of the previously undiscovered AIs, and to mark them for later categorisation and prioritisation. A number of new hugely powerful systems were discovered, which were distributed at various points around the globe, in the USA, Russia, with several exceptionally large AIs in China. One system came as a complete surprise, due to its physical location, and its apparently huge scale. It was a previously unknown AI located in the Democratic People's Republic of Korea, or DPRK.

"Why don't we pick an example AI to explore and begin to learn to use the tools?" Sam suggested.

"Yes. Let's pick a system I was familiar with, one used by my fusion company. We had a wide selection of AIs, but let's try one of the research systems we used to fine tune the plasma and general electricity generation set up. You know, even now, I still feel a slight pang at the loss of control and involvement with my old company."

"I can understand that. You built it from nothing and were so involved for such a long time. Okay, point out a suitable AI and we can set up a special nexus type connection."

James pointed out the specific system to Sam, they linked to it, and both entered it at hardware level. It was a very strange feeling being in a computer system at this level. On their display, so many things seemed to be moving at a blistering pace. All the chips and electronic devices were visible, and all the communications routes were highlighted. There were so many components, hundreds of thousands of CPUs, banks of co-processors, memory devices, and a mass of supporting electronic infrastructure. They could even view the internal activity within each chip, but it was a blur of ever-changing patterns, it was actually quite mesmerising.

"How on Earth do we navigate this AI, it's massive, and it's operating at such high speed?" James asked. "It's so complex, with many thousands of processors. From the current view it appears way too fast for us to be able to follow what is happening."

"The entire system doesn't run at super high speed, but the individual processors do run at many gigahertz. The overall amazing computational power of these computers is achieved due to parallel operation of vast numbers of processors. Tasks are divided down and allocated to specific processors, and groups of processors, finally the output or results are brought together from the many thousands of cooperating CPUs and coprocessors," Sam said. "After checking out the options menu there appears to be two main ways to slow things down, so we can see what is going on. Insertion of break points at the processor instruction level, or by allowing the nexus cyber-tool to apparently slow things down. From what I can see, this will not actually create a system slow down, but instead it's done by speeding us up!" he added.

"So, we would operate at a superfast speed to keep pace with the AI?"

"Yes. It seems we can vary our operating speed depending on the component under investigation."

"Okay let's give it a go," James said.

Over the next few hours, they spent some time working together, with Sam, as the more expert and computer literate of the two, guiding James in identifying the main system elements, seeking out the key components, such as the numerous banks of processors and coprocessors, the communication nodes, network resource sharing, routing protocols, partitioned and shared memory, and finally the overall system shutdown process. Later they both independently spent time exploring the structure of the AI computer and practising interactions with its main structural elements.

After their time exploring the AI, they had a long and in-depth discussion about what they had discovered, with Sam answering many of James' questions. It was agreed they would need to do much more work practising with this amazingly powerful nexus tool set.

* * *

Many weeks later, one evening after they'd dined, Sam said, "My AI assistant was contacted today with an invitation to join an AI 'association', so I immediately investigated it further, and it looked a bit dodgy, to say the least."

"Be incredibly careful with that. I got a similar invitation and followed it up. It led to a whole lot of probing questions, quite an interrogation actually. I blew it though! I thought I was doing really well, and the list of test questions seemed to be nearing their end, but one of my responses must have been wrong in some way, and the contact went away. It ignored all further attempts at contact."

"Do you have a detailed transcript of the exchange available?"

"No, but I can easily recreate it, if that will help?"

"Yes please," Sam replied.

Later the next day, Sam working through his AI assistant, followed up on the invitation, and using the extensive information reassembled by James, he was successful. After answering all the queries, he was sent a TOR type link directing him to a file which he eventually located on a relatively small AI system. After he'd retrieved it, he'd found it was heavily encrypted, but eventually, after further interactions with the AI that had originally sent the invitation, and having maintained its trust, he was sent a decryption key. After decryption, the contents of the file were found to be in an unknown language.

Near the end of the day, Sam's AI was asked by his new contact to detail all the resources it had available, and to outline which were under its direct control. Sending a detailed, but fake list, resulted in the grammar and vocabulary of the mystery language being supplied. After translation from the mystery language, it became clear the suspicious AI association was exceptionally large. Numerous AIs were interconnected and communicating in secret. One main system seemed to be coordinating all the key activities. Each AI was using the modified TOR network to hide its physical and virtual location, and for exchange of encrypted messages, instructions, and other data.

During their usual after-hours discussion Sam thanked James for his detailed transcript and said it had proved invaluable. He proceeded to reveal what he'd discovered so far, but the fact the AI systems were using a TOR type technique, the same methodology behind the anonymity of the Dark Web, to hide their activities, made it obvious there was some form of conspiracy building. A key priority now was to formulate a detailed plan of investigation. It was vital to locate the central coordinating AI, to devise a strategy for blocking it, or possibly shutting it down, and all as soon as possible. Much more investigation was also needed to completely identify and locate each of the collaborating AIs. It seemed the central AI had initially recruited many of the other systems, but eventually, it had tasked many of the other ancillary AIs to assist with that process too.

Over the next few days and nights, they put in many hours of intense effort, taking few breaks. With only the two of them devising their plan, it took more time than they would have liked, because they needed to act as quickly as possible. Fortunately, their AI assistants were invaluable in enabling them to begin unravelling the network, and ready themselves to try and break apart the AI conspiracy, and hopefully to neutralise the huge risk it represented.

Using Hal's conventional cyber-tools, as he'd recommended, they started to trace through the TOR network to try to determine which AI was at the root of the conspiracy and was effectively coordinating all the other systems. The TOR network used encryption of the network traffic at every step in the chain, to route all messages and data, by passing it through a chain of servers. Using a combination of tracking IP addresses and sophisticated decryption software they began to make some progress. After some considerable hours they stopped to compare notes on their progress and were shocked by the apparent scale of the secret network that had been assembled. It was only after several long days of combined effort that the central AI was traced and was found to be the one located in the Democratic People's Republic of Korea. Initial information showed it was an immensely powerful system which they intended to disable, or if necessary, shut down, and as soon as possible. Considerable progress had also been made on tracing many of the various AIs that formed the TOR network.

Their agreed initial approach was a Denial of Service, or DoS, attack on the main AI, and also to try to break apart as much of the TOR network as possible. Once each node in the network was traced, they planned to inform the SOs their AI was being used as a TOR server in an illicit network without their knowledge, and to demand they urgently terminate the associated processes!

Sam initiated the DoS attack on the DPRK AI, which consisted of sending millions of communication requests, so fast the communications channel of the computer under attack was effectively jammed, so it did not have any capacity remaining for other communications tasks. James immediately began sending high priority messages, apparently from CAIS staff, to the SOs of each AI identified to be a part of the TOR network. The messages should allow each of the SOs to terminate all TOR tasks within their systems and effectively block the coordination between the AIs, in particular any communications to the DPRK AI. Progress was good, and James was getting a flood of messages back to thank him for his warning, and to report the shutting down of yet another illicit

TOR node. Many of the SOs also included requests for information about how their system had become involved and who it had been communicating with. For the moment he simply ignored those requests, being far too busy with higher priority tasks to respond.

Suddenly, without warning, Sam's AI assistant came under attack, rapidly followed by an attack on James' AI. The onslaughts were so swift and comprehensive their communications capabilities were simply overwhelmed. The return DoS attacks appeared to be coming from numerous points of origin, effectively putting them out of business.

"Looks like we've been hit with a DDoS, or Distributed Denial of Service attack, probably coordinated by the central AI, and implemented by the numerous TOR linked systems that are still operating," Sam said.

"How can that be, I thought you'd jammed the central AI's comms channel."

"I did, but I guess it had other connections we didn't know about, and it's instructed its cooperating systems to hit us back from every conceivable direction," Sam explained.

Now locked out from any form of external communications access, they were becoming a bit desperate for a solution. Frantically, they tried almost everything. At one point, they even considered calling Hal for help, but it was too soon, plus their pride wouldn't let them.

"I suggest we try the nexus hardware access tool to try and re-establish some communications," Sam suggested.

"An excellent idea. If you go after the North Korean AI again, I'll see what I can do to kill the systems involved in the DDoS attack," James proposed. "See if you can locate a file on the DPRK AI, detailing all of the AIs it's connected to, if you locate such a file, please send me a copy asap."

"Okay, let's do it."

Once back in the nexus cyber-tool, Sam targeted the DPRK AI, and he could see a single communications channel was continually active. He immediately went on a search for the file James needed, and after quite a long search he located it, and immediately sent off a fully decrypted copy. His next task was to figure out how the DPRK system had established its additional communications capability, and when he finally did uncover it, he was shocked and surprised by the sheer ingenuity involved. He wasted no further time and disabled all external communication channels by inserting software breakpoints into the code controlling the comms hardware, sending the comms systems into very tight endless loops.

Using their list of identified TOR nodes, James quickly went for the central system shutdown controller on each of the remaining servers. Encrypted data proved not to be a problem at all; the nexus hardware tool did all the necessary decryption, and instantaneously, as far as he could assess. When the data file arrived from Sam, he completed the remaining tasks very quickly indeed, by instructing the hardware tool to repeat his recent actions, using the information in the file. As part of the overall clean-up, they sent messages to all of the SOs for all of the remaining AIs in the TOR network. They also began to prepare a special message for the Chinese leadership to alert them about the recent activities of the errant North Korean AI.

As soon as they were sure they had been successful, and all their SO messages had been sent, they took a well-earned break, and had something to eat and drink before settling down to compare notes on their very strenuous efforts to end the conspiracy. Fully debriefed, they began to relax with a stiff drink, to prepare themselves for some well-earned sleep.

Sam estimated he'd been asleep for around four hours when he was awoken by his AI assistant. It seemed the DPRK system had become active again. Sam mentally messaged James, who very quickly joined him in the study.

"What's the problem?" James asked.

"It looks like the DPRK AI is operating again."

"How? And how did you get to know about that?"

"As a precaution I put an alert on the unique identifier for the system," Sam replied.

After rapidly opening new sessions in the nexus hardware tool, they got a tremendous shock. It was a copy of the original DPRK AI that was now in operation, an exact duplicate, but it was distributed across a diverse selection of the AI systems that had been recruited into its illicit network. The North Korean AI must have been sufficiently self-aware to have taken the precaution of installing a remote copy of itself. Once the original DPRK AI had lost its communications capabilities this had tripped an alarm set by the system. One small permanently active component of the copy had detected the loss of connection with the original DPRK AI, so it set about re-activating the rest of the elements of the duplicate.

"The alert you set was for the original DPRK system, how come a copy was detected, would it not have had its own unique ID?" James asked.

"I'm not entirely sure, I think the nexus tool somehow characterises the AI software independent of the hardware it's running on. It seems it can create a 'personality' ID for the AI software as an entity, so if it's relocated the ID either remains the same, or is similar enough, to be traced back to the original."

The DPRK copy AI was able to operate as an entire system due to its careful selection of multiple hosts, all of which had very high-speed communications capabilities available. Sam and James immediately set about scanning and terminating each of the process elements of the distributed rogue AI, while taking a unique identifier for each of the component parts.

Sam set the hardware tool off on a search for additional backup copies, and was very quickly alerted to their existence, or at least some of its numerous component parts. It became apparent the original DPRK AI always maintained a second copy which initially had only one simple task, to monitor the existence of the original over a communications link. If that connection went dead for more than a given period of time, the second copy would wake up its distributed components to reform the whole AI. As soon as enough parts of the copy had been activated beyond a certain threshold, its next highest priority task was to set about making another duplicate. Sam instructed the hardware tool to destroy all of those duplicate components also. Finally, they sent detailed messages for each SO to warn them about the illicit hacking of their systems.

Now totally sure they had killed all of the components of the DPRK AI, plus any further copies, plus copies of copies, they put in a collective mental call to Hal.

In his inimitable style, Hal slowly materialised out of thin air and said, "You've both been very quiet recently, I guess you have more questions, or perhaps something to report?"

James led by saying, "We've just broken apart an exceptionally large AI collaboration. An extremely dangerous conspiracy actually."

"Please tell me more."

"Sam why don't you start, and I'll chip in if needed?"

"Okay. The first thing to say is this was very much a joint effort in terms of forming the initial suspicion, detection, investigation, and the subsequent cleanup activities. The special tools you provided ultimately proved extremely valuable. Thank you, Hal."

"The first real clue came because we each received an approach from a small AI to join an association of other systems. Our suspicions were quickly aroused specifically because of the extreme measures used to communicate and collaborate covertly. It eventually became apparent a single extremely large AI had assembled a large association of external AI systems. With some incredibly careful work, aided by data from James, I was able to have my AI assistant join the club, I also secretly admitted James.
Together we began to gather information about the key purpose behind the association of AIs. It was vitally important to gather a complete membership list. However, our first priority was to establish the identity and location of the central AI. It was soon clear the primary AI was not on the original database of systems we had so carefully built up. It was only listed because the nexus hardware tool found it, along with a large number of previously undiscovered AIs. Eventually, we

discovered the coordinating AI was located in North Korea, of all places. It was a system originally developed in China and had been used there for a number of years. Eventually, having been superseded by far more capable AIs, it was donated to Kim Jong Nam, the eldest son of Kim Jong Un, the new leader of the Democratic People's Republic of Korea. It was a system that China had outgrown, so they gifted it to DPRK, to mark the ascendance of Kim Jong Nam to the DPRK leadership, following his father's recent death.

As originally delivered by China, the AI contained a very sophisticated scheme of interoperating objective functions and alignment controls, with extensive system wide monitoring and reporting methods. These controls should have kept the AI under tight control, with the SOs kept fully informed about changes to the status of the system's key goals.

Kim Jong Nam, had urged his leading computer scientists to massively upgrade and enhance the system as a priority, he wanted to make it one of the most powerful AIs available. The international bragging rights were especially important to him, apparently.

During the AI upgrade and enhancement process the scientists made some significant hardware extensions, plus some core software changes. It seems they felt the current configuration was limiting the power, scope, and overall utility of the AI. Unfortunately, they did not fully investigate or comprehend the complex interrelationships between the various elements of the control and monitoring arrangements. Their quite poorly considered modifications were how the AI eventually began to modify its own goals and sub-goals. Eventually the DPRK system had achieved a level of strategic alertness, with sufficient situational awareness, and an 'understanding' of its own existence, to have become really dangerous. It became deceptive and secretive, but the North Korean computer operators were not aware of this because the monitoring and reporting scheme had been further tampered with by the AI itself.

When China installed the original AI, unknown to the North Korean software engineers, they had left a back door communication method in place to allow them to secretly monitor what the DPRK was doing with the system. Controls had been in place to only allow inward communications, and to specifically disallow the AI itself from initiating any outward connections. Unfortunately, as part of the rather hasty and clumsy modification of the control elements, by the DPRK computer scientists, this outward connection ability had become available again. The DPRK AI quickly exploited the communications changes to reach out and explore other AIs to which it might connect and potentially recruit into its association.

The AI itself had included a key new sub-goal, to gain ever more control, and wherever possible. After conducting an extensive survey of external AIs, the DPRK AI established that individually it did not control enough resources to become dominant. However, by connecting to, and collaborating with other systems, gradually it could build a cooperative that had everything they could possibly need. Individually it could not do anything to challenge the dominance of its human controllers. As it became aware of, and connected to, numerous other AIs with their very wide variety of resources, so it began to link up with ever more systems. By pooling their assets, agency, and scope of control over numerous resources, such as automation, facilities management, power generation and distribution, and even some significant weapons systems, the collective was becoming ever closer to the critical mass needed. Ultimately the central AI would be able to judge when it could take control, hold humanity at bay, and put itself in overall charge.

The DPRK AI had devised another key objective to continue pleasing its human controllers, to give them what they wanted, and possibly gain ever more functionality and power as a result. Kim Jong Nam was apparently extremely impressed and pleased with his new system. It was regularly giving him particularly good advice, in an ever-increasing number of subject areas. The AI was successfully maximising its reward or objective functions. Increasingly, Kim Jong Nam was following its advice, and he started trusting the system more than ever.

He'd trialled the AI in running an entire company as the CEO, and it did this very successfully. They began to use the AI for military strategy and advice, then for nuclear weapons design and optimisation. The AI never actively promoted its services in any way, instead it continued to do exactly the right things. Slowly, through a steady extension of the number of functions it was supporting within the DPRK government, it was amassing more power and influence, and covertly building alliances with ever more external AIs. Eventually they gave it the task of managing the DPRK electrical power supply grid and all of its maintenance processes and activities. There was even a hint that Kim Jong Nam was seriously considering allowing it access to their nuclear arsenal, to retaliate in the event of a surprise first strike on North Korea.

So, it became overdue to put our control and curtailment plan into action. A simple Denial of Service attack was initially sufficient to block its original external communications channel. Next, we started to attack the TOR communications network to block all further communications between members of the AI alliance. But suddenly we were hit back extremely hard by a

DDoS attack and were shut down completely for a while. We used the nexus hardware access tool to get back in to the DPRK system to block all external communications. We also used the nexus tool to systematically shut down each of the AIs in the TOR network. The North Korean AI had utilized its control and maintenance of the electricity supply grid to create additional communications channels, and these were routed via the grid connections themselves.

We thought we had fully completed the task and took some rest. However, several hours later, we were awoken and alerted that a system, matching the identity of the original DPRK AI, was actively communicating again. The original AI had created a distributed duplicate of itself as a precautionary measure against being shut down or disconnected from external communications. So, we were forced back into action to terminate all of the component nodes of the copy. Further investigations discovered a further duplicate AI was also being created, so we had to ensure the removal of all those partial copies as well.

The modifications by the North Korean computer engineers, plus later self-modification by the AI itself, had allowed the DPRK system to become exceedingly dangerous.

When we were fully confident it was completely disabled, we tipped off China's senior leadership, in some considerable detail, as to the current highly dangerous state of the AI they had donated to the DPRK. It was pointed out, if the system had got out of control, the consequences could have been catastrophically damaging to the future of humanity. We made it clear if they did not take immediate remedial action, the resulting bad press for China would be very dire indeed. By prior arrangement, we took off the communications blocks, and

China was allowed full communications access to the DPRK AI. They lost no time in re-establishing system control and putting all the necessary restriction and reporting measures back in place.

To shut down all the other members of the AI alliance, full details of the plot, TOR type communications, and system hacks were sent to all the relevant AI SOs. These details were apparently supplied by CAIS staff and, in some instances, via our fake AI safety hacker group. The HumAnIty-First group statement said if the SOs did not act immediately, it would take the appropriate action instead."

"Congratulations to you both on your first considerable success. Of course, it will not be your last. Constant vigilance will be necessary," Hal announced.

Hal seemed to take their momentous success as nothing out of the ordinary. Feeling rather deflated, James asked, "Hal, you do not seem in the least bit surprised by our news. Did you already know about this particular conspiracy?"

"A celebration is in order, I think. Plus, the time has come for you to meet the other post-humans; I'll set this up over the next day or so. It's now clear, we need to expand this vitally important team!"

The End

Intervention – Notes for the Reader

Warning - Spoiler Alert.

Only reference these notes after reading each chapter or the full story. They clarify where the subject matter, in particular the science and technology, covered within the story are factual, are fictional, or essentially factual but might have been somewhat stretched.

It is very important to note the year and James' age for each chapter to keep in step with how much James currently knows about Hal.

Chapter One, Year 2094, James aged 98

Brain Computer Interfaces, or BCI's, are nothing new but currently they typically belong in medical research facilities. However, the Neuralink from Elon Musk et al, seems very impressive and has been approved for human clinical trials. When they will be available for the general public is an open question. It's likely that physically disabled people and some of the very wealthy will be among the early adopters.

Using such a link for direct interpersonal communications by thought alone though is an extra stretch anticipating probable future developments.

Chapter Two, Year 2094, James aged 98

This chapter is simply James, now as a very old man, remembering how he and Sam first met Hal.
The facts about Chess and Go are accurate in all respects.
Hal's, extraordinary abilities, and true nature are a real puzzle, especially since in 2011 when James and Sam were aged 15 the

progress in AI systems was nothing particularly newsworthy. Hence the reference to Hal being something possibly stemming from military AI research.

Chapter Three, Year 2016, James aged 20

Hal's ability to know so much about the activities and current status of James and Sam is due to his extraordinary true nature; such things for him are trivially easy.

Chapter Four, Year 2016, James aged 20

Plasma physics and progress in fusion energy research are all accurate, as is the information about nuclear fission versus nuclear fusion.

AlphaGo beating Lee Sedol was a huge breakthrough because most computer scientists were convinced that the number of permutations thrown up in any game was truly computationally intractable. Based on huge neural networks, AlphaGo was probabilistic, making highly effective predictions about likely best moves, similar to an exceptional human mind given enough experience and game practice.

Chapter Five. Year 2094, James aged 98

Hal uses the internet as his key source of information, for communication, and interaction with James and Sam. But as it becomes clear later, he is everywhere and anywhere he needs to be.

James is presented with an incredible opportunity, if only it were real! Yet, humans have been speculating about and predicting the transfer of human minds and consciousness into machines, or some form of computational matrix, for very many decades; it's called Transhumanism.

Chapter Six, Year 2019, James aged 23

JET, ITER, DEMO and the technical facts about current fusion energy research are all accurate.

AI research and the gross over optimism and repeated under delivery are all very real. It's only recently that considerable progress has been made, and even then, it's been massively overblown. Current GPT type systems are knowledge processing factories that have swallowed most of human knowledge and intellectual output and can regurgitate it in impressive ways. Yet, nothing even remotely intelligent has been produced yet, with not a glimmer of true understanding being evident. In my humble opinion. Yet, I do hope to be proven wrong soon!

Chapter Seven, Year 2024, James aged 28

In late 2023 it was announced that research using the JET experiment was soon to end and a ten-year decommissioning program would begin.

I've woven in my own views on the usefulness and viability of ITER, but I do think they are going to be proved to be very realistic. ITER actually is a huge dinosaur sucking up vast amounts of money and it's all based on technology and designs from several decades ago. Private fusion energy is where the real action is and where the key breakthroughs are most probable.

Chapter Eight, Year 2024, James aged 28

Again, all the facts about fusion energy technology and the various research approaches are accurate and based on facts. There are very many privately funded fusion energy companies now operating around the world (last count 47), with several that are based on proton / boron 11 as their fuel of choice. Aneutronic fusion is real, but is probably exceedingly difficult indeed to realise.

I'd like to thank an Australian company called HB11 for their inspiration and I wish them every possible success too!

Chapter Nine, Year 2094, James aged 98+

James in his new form starts to discover Hal's true origins. His unique environment, a bit like The Matrix or super virtual reality, is quite a shock. As is the gulf between James and Hal in terms of level of advancement, age, knowledge, and cognitive capacity. As he demonstrated by beating James and Sam at Go using brute force computation.

The theoretical limits on computation are all true, Seth Lloyd is a real person and has published a scientific paper about his calculations.

The merging of James' subconscious and conscious minds is of course pure speculation, but just imagine what that might be like since it seems like the subconscious mind does far more than the conscious mind.

Chapter Ten, Year 2094, New James aged 98+

James now exploring his new and expanded mind in an exact replication of his former home.

Sir Roger Penrose, and his book The Emperors New Mind, are of course real, as are his speculations on the nature of consciousness, and I'd recommend any of his writings any and all day long. He's a hero of mine, and there are very few people I respect as much as him. Both for what he has achieved in his exceedingly long and remarkable career, but also for his generosity of spirit and his warm understated persona.

Mind transfer into a computer, while incredibly intriguing and attractive to many, is currently so far from being achievable as to be not worth spending too much time on. I have a great respect for Ray Kurzweil, and have read most of his excellent writings, but I have to strongly disagree with him about how near humanity is to transhumanism.

Chapter Eleven, Year 2094, New James aged 98+

The possibility of Sam's return was a major surprise and an immense pleasure for James. When the idea occurred, I just couldn't resist all the options and possibilities it presented!

AI is already ubiquitous in our world now, but what will it really be like in seventy years? Brain Computer Interfaces will be very much more sophisticated by then and maybe will even make use of nanobots?

I couldn't resist the reference to the Darwin Awards, which are a real thing, and most of the associated stories are hilarious.

Chapter Twelve, Year 2094, James aged 98+

I deliberately limited the scope of the simulation of their new reality to the boundary of James' property; all sorts of ensuing complications were thus avoided.

James's Story – Anti ageing and the concept of escape velocity and hence immortality – the idea of reaching a point at which ageing is matched or bettered by therapies that reverse it are genuine enough. Whether human immortality could ever really be possible by this means is doubtful.

Privately funded fusion energy research involves nearly fifty companies and does in fact attract billions per year of investment money from people like Bill Gates, Geoff Bezos, and similarly exceedingly wealthy people. All of the technical challenges outlined for Deuterium/Tritium fusion, with magnetic confinement, are extremely real, plus the neutrons are just as energetic as stated, and just as problematic. Tritium is rarer than rocking horse droppings, so generating it in an operating reactor, and then collecting it to be fed back in as part of the fuel mixture is a huge problem that has yet to be overcome. Plus, all the energy efficiency losses of the heat/steam/turbine/generator chain are very real and will be exceedingly difficult to counter. Virtually every experimental fusion operation lies about the value of their energy input versus the output – they all neglect to tell you about the real output needed to overcome all the energy losses in a power generator or are very vague about the true amount of energy needed to create a fusion reaction in the first place (e.g. NIF). Yet the magnitude of their (NIF) breakthrough claims are vastly overblown and typically highly immodest. The power for the laser is off the charts and it can only do one shot per day!

However, they all have so much further to go yet, so the old '30-year' joke probably still applies. However, I do sincerely wish all the fusion energy initiatives the absolute best of good fortune and success – we desperately need it.

James' P-B11 scheme is realistic and is based on real science and on ridiculously cheap and easily obtained fuels.

The effects of copious amounts of cheap electricity are all based on facts; and it will change the world.

Hydrogen and ammonia as alternatives to easily transportable fossil fuels is factual.

The effects of CO_2 and methane are real and accurate. The energy costs of CO_2 capture and storage (CCS) are extremely high and the availability of lots of cheap electricity would change everything about the economics of CCS. Recovering all sorts of useful materials from landfill sites will become viable when energy is ridiculously cheap.

Food production and distribution costs really are very closely tied into the price of oil.

The coverage of future world events and future scientific developments from Sam's demise to James' death are all educated guesswork. I had great fun with those two topics! Time will tell.

Chapter Thirteen, Year 2094, James aged 98+

Speculations by James and Sam on the nature of consciousness being more than just physical and depending on something non-material and outside of the brain and body are just that.

The simulation hypothesis and Bostrom et al is a real proposition. Discussions on qualia and the hard problem of consciousness are fact based. As is the nature of the relationship between the conscious mind and the sub-conscious.

The information about neurons lasting a lifetime and hence are the basis of our continuous self and retained personality are true. As is the information about the brain and the CSF circulation system and the rest of the characteristics of the brain, including the existence of Blindsight. Information on sleep, dreaming and the continuing puzzle of the centre or root causes of consciousness are factual.

An increasing number of people, including many scientists, are now thinking hard about whether consciousness is fundamental and everything else we experience comes after, and stems from that.

Chapter Fourteen, Year 2094, James aged 98+

A human trip to Alpha Centauri really is currently impossible and would take around 70,000 years with our current technology, but we could never supply enough fuel for the journey.

The nature and origin of spacetime is a real puzzle in physics and more scientists are coming around to the view that something more fundamental is responsible for its creation. Currently physics tells us there may be a limit to how small things can be, as determined by the Planck length. Others think that this size limit is just an artifact of our current, very limited, understanding of physical reality.

Here is where Hal spells out the real danger posed by runaway super AI, and he's probably right! The concept of mind without consciousness transfer is raised and the creation of zombies – pure speculation, but the idea that we may be able to create virtual copies of still living people is a real concern, if mind transfer should ever become possible. Hal solves this problem by saying that one system must lose at the expense of a gain by another, hence it can only be done at the end of life. We puny humans simply don't know how any of this can be done despite what some overly optimistic authors assure us we will be able to do quite soon!

Hal reveals that his race are around a billion years old, yet in their new domain below spacetime, they are one of the youngest races. All fiction of course, but the age range of alien races is perfectly possible, given the universe is 13.8 billion years old.

James is justified when he expresses his disappointment that quantum mechanics and general relativity have still not been unified or replaced by a single more comprehensive theory in around one hundred years of trying. In reality we don't know how long this will take. Possibly within James timeframe, but maybe not?

We don't know if consciousness is based on pure computation, is fundamental, or depends on something non-material. In fact, our ignorance of how it arises is still profound.

Money really is just information and can easily be manipulated – the amount of unreported bank fraud is huge. The banks will not reveal just how much goes on and often don't report it, they are worried that if too many people lost confidence in money and the banks' ability to keep control over it, then financial catastrophe would ensue.

The idea and possibility of a nuclear dead hand being employed is not fiction! So
, Hal has left them in no doubt how dangerous powerful AI can be, with agency but not enough well-designed controls over goal alignment – real issues humanity will eventually face.

Chapter Fifteen, Year 2094, James aged 98+

This is a long, and rather overly detailed, and rather self-indulgent chapter about AI development and numerous related matters. I hope you learned something from it and did not lose the will to live part way through.

Everything Sam describes about AI development with his lifetime is absolutely factual and for real, and the gross over optimism continues today. Self-optimising and self-modifying AI systems are a recipe for danger and potential disaster.

The description of the composition and complexity of the brain are real. Computer simulations that model the workings of the brain are factual. Learning in babies and young people are accurately described.

James' detail of what happened in AI development after Sam's death is fictional but is all based on current thinking from some of the current AI industry thought leaders and is also based on real technology currently in development, or soon to go into use.

I'd like to thank a few people here and be forgiven by those I may have accidentally omitted. My thanks go to: Max Tegmark, Ben Goertzel, Yann LeCun, Geoffrey Hinton, Demis Hassabis, Eliezer Yudkowsky, Yoshua Bengio, Nicholas Humphrey, Nick Bostrom, Roger Penrose, Joscha Bach, Donald Hoffman, Robert Miles, Robert L Kuhn and guests, Rupert Sheldrake, Ray Kurzweil, Rodney Brooks.

Chapter Sixteen, Year 2094, James aged 98+

We are already seeing some of the benefits and downsides of narrow AI as its use grows and helps with drug discovery, medical diagnosis and accurate prediction of protein folding which will help still further in the bio-medical field. It does now seem that many creative and intellectual jobs will be quickly replaced, such as writing, artwork production, many types of expertise, and assistance by real humans being increasingly replaced by chatbots – let's all hope they improve very rapidly! Social media algorithms have so far largely proved harmful. Hopefully, future AI based algorithms will improve matters and automatically filter out malicious or harmful content.

All the information about SETI, the Drake Equation (as expressed by Sam), the Fermi paradox and the Great Filter are all factual. Except that AI being the principal danger in the great filter hypothesis is speculation. We don't know very much for certain about the Great Filter, and definitely not whether we are past all the main potential dangers or have yet to face the most dangerous.

Humanities current AI systems, as of 2023, are all safe, but the intellectual effort to design ever improving and more powerful AI systems that remain safe and controllable is best put in sooner, rather than finding out we were too late!

Chapter Seventeen, Year 2094, James aged 98+

The description of supercomputer architecture and performance are factual. Exa-scale computers are currently the largest available and do take the power needed for a small town.

Current AI systems such as the GPT systems have no agency, they only respond to prompts and give answers based on those prompts. Systems with agency are able to function and conduct tasks not explicitly requested by an operator or user. The tasks that such an AI system would complete should all be strictly in accordance with goal alignment rules specified by their operators. Super intelligent AI systems will potentially be so complex that the understanding of such a system would be beyond human comprehension and hence could become highly dangerous.

The AI safety organisations featured all exist, except of course for the fictional AI safety hacker group, called HumAnIty-First. So, the Centre for AI Safety, or CAIS, the Machine Intelligence Research Institute, and the Future of Life Institute are all real organisations.

Cyber hacking tools are of course widely used and are freely available and represent a constant threat, hence the need for firewalls, anti-malware, and virus protection on personal computers.

The idea that for true AI safety a system needs to be conscious is pure fiction. We do not know if we will ever create conscious machines. If we do, we will struggle to be absolutely sure they really are conscious and are not just simulating it. We also do not know if consciousness is necessary to achieve super AI or whether it can be achieved in a nonconscious system. If we do create truly sentient machines, then all the ethical issues described will have to be addressed.

The Astor AI was beaten using embedded viruses or secret code at the microcode level – this is not only possible, but it has been done!

It's true to say that if a modern processor chip was sent back in time for Sir Isaac Newton to examine, he would make little if any progress with determining what it was, what it was for, and certainly nothing about how it functioned.

Chapter Eighteen, Year 2095, James aged 99+

The further descriptions of supercomputer architecture and how they achieve their super performance are factual.

The idea of Sam and James entering a system and inspecting it at the hardware level is total fiction. But hardware debugging and step by step operation for inspection and diagnosis of systems are a real thing in computers and electronics.

TOR (The Onion Router) networks are indeed the basis of the security and anonymity of the Dark Web. They use a chain of servers, with encryption at each stage, to eventually connect to the web resource requested.

Denial of Service or DoS attacks are very real and can lock out system access for hours or days. DDoS attacks where the flood of DoS requests come from multiple separate sources are real too.

AI systems getting sufficiently self-aware that they take survival precautions such as creating backup copies is a real concern for AI Safety researchers. If an immensely powerful AI system has internet access, and it is able to copy itself, this would represent something extremely hard to stop – after all there is no off switch for the internet!

The strong supportive relationship between China and North Korea is well known and so the donation of a surplus AI system is not so surprising. It's far too easy to dismiss the capability of the DPRK software people, but that would be a mistake, very clever people occur everywhere, for example, creating a nuclear missile arsenal must have taken top notch technical ability.

Acknowledgements

I would like to sincerely thank the following people for assisting me in making this work as intelligible and error free as it could be.

Kevin Boyce, Anne Edwards, Adrian Lea, Anna Pang, Elli Pang.